# Piper

## NATALE GHENT

ORCA BOOK PUBLISHERS

**National Library of Canada cataloguing in publication data**
Ghent, Natale, 1962–
Piper

ISBN 1-55143-167-X

I. Title.
PS8563.H46P56 2000   jC813'.6   C00-910884-X
PZ7-G3390235Pi 2000

First published in the United States, 2001

**Library of Congress Catalog Card Number:** 00-107535

Orca Book Publishers gratefully acknowledges the support for our publishing programs provided by the following agencies: The Government of Canada through the Book Publishing Industry Development Program (BPIDP), The Canada Council for the Arts, and the British Columbia Arts Council.

Cover illustration by Ljuba Levstek
Interior illustrations by Cindy Ghent
Cover design by Christine Toller
Printed and bound in Canada

**IN CANADA:**
**Orca Book Publishers**
PO Box 5626, Station B
Victoria, BC  Canada
V8R 6S4

**IN THE UNITED STATES:**
**Orca Book Publishers**
PO Box 468
Custer, WA  USA
98240-0468

03 02 01  •  5 4 3 2

*To Wesley. I love you.*

I would like to thank my family, who read all my stories with unwavering enthusiasm: Mom, Rita, Cindy, Monika, Wesley, Cassel, Hayden, Jasmine, Norman, Franz and especially Mark. Thanks to my editor, Andrew Wooldridge, for his patience and honesty. Thanks to Jim Murphy and my pals Dom, Chris and Richard for being there for me, and to my best friend Cath for unbridled conversations over coffee and chocolate torte. And a special thank you to Colin, for watching over me.

*From the frozen hills behind the little farm, the haunting cries of coyotes echo in the dark. The sheep dog sniffs the air, shifting nervously in the whelping pen. She circles several times, then lies down with a low, satisfied grunt. She is safe tonight. Safe from the cold and hunger that bite relentlessly at the heels of the coyotes in the black woods. Safe to rest and wait for the arrival of her puppies.*

# 1.

## STORM BREWING

 The girls tried to be good, but the thrill of actually seeing the puppies made them forget their promise. For months before this night, they dreamed of what the puppies would be like. In blanketed whispers they imagined their numbers, the color of their fur, how many girls there would be, and how many boys. Tonight they would discover what months of dreaming could not reveal. It was hard not to be too excited.

"That ain't the right towel, Wesley," Cassel scolded her cousin who stood on a chair in front of the linen closet in the upstairs hall.

"Isn't," Wesley corrected her.

"That's what I said," Cassel snapped.

"This *is* the right towel," Wesley snapped back.

"It's the red one — just like your mom said."

"My mom said the *old* red towel. That's one of the newer ones. Get off the chair and let me get it." Cassel moved as though to stand on the chair.

"I can find it, Cassel. It's just a stupid towel. Give me a chance." She held one arm out, preventing her cousin from getting on the chair.

"You're taking too long!" Cassel flared. "Holly will have her puppies by the time you find it." She knocked Wesley's hand out of the way then shoved at her legs.

Wesley careened to the edge of the chair, rocked forward to regain her balance, then tumbled to the wooden floor in a loud and angry heap. "You little witch!" she screamed. "I'm going to kill you!" She sprang at her cousin, her blue eyes flashing with rage. But before she could even reach her, Cassel let out an ear-piercing shriek, disarming Wesley in midattack.

"What's all the hullabaloo?!" Aunt Cindy yelled from the foot of the stairs.

"Wesley tried to kill me!" Cassel shouted.

"Cassel pushed me off the chair!"

"Good Lord!" Aunt Cindy sighed with exasperation. "I asked you girls to get a towel. If you can't even do that without fighting, you may as well both go to bed and forget about helping with the puppies!"

"But, Mom!" Cassel protested. "She wasn't getting the *right* towel. You said you wanted the old red one 'cause that's the one you use for whelping."

"She didn't give me a chance." Wesley flew to her own defense.

Aunt Cindy held up her hands as she climbed the stairs. "I don't want to hear it."

Rosemary appeared at the foot of the stairs. "What on earth is going on?"

"Oh nothing, Mom — just Cassel trying to break my neck!" Wesley shouted.

"I did not! You weren't getting the right towel," Cassel insisted. "She never does anything right!" She turned to Wesley, sneering. "Why don't you go back to California and leave us alone!"

Wesley looked at Cassel in shock. She didn't speak, but lunged at her cousin, catching her by the braid and slapping wildly at her face.

"Girls!" Rosemary gasped.

The cousins scratched and clawed at each other.

Aunt Cindy charged up the stairs and grabbed them forcibly by the backs of their shirts, pulling them apart and shaking them the way she would one of her dogs who had misbehaved. "That's it," she hissed through clenched teeth. "You can both cool off in your room and just forget about helping with the puppies. I'm sick and tired of this endless fighting!"

Cassel turned to protest, but her mother jerked her around, pushing the girls into their bedroom and closing the door with a slam.

"Way to go, Wesley," Cassel jeered.

"Don't even look at me, or you'll regret it," Wesley seethed, the waves of anger washing over her.

Cassel stared back defiantly, her ice blue eyes filled with contempt, her normally pale face flushed and red on the side where Wesley had hit her. She tossed her head imperiously, then flounced over to her side of the bedroom, collapsing on her bed with an arrogant sniff. She knew better than to push the situation. As daring as she was, she knew that Wesley could get the better of her when she was angry. She furrowed her brow, pressing her face against the frosted glass of the window at the foot of her bed. Her two stubby braids stuck out from the back of her head like the velvet horns of a young goat.

Wesley sat on her own bed, leaning against the wall, glowering at her younger cousin. I hate her, she thought. I hate her face and everything about her! If she so much as looks at me, I'll make her sorry. Seeing those puppies born was the only thing worth living for around here and now I don't even get to do that!

She bit her nails, her blue eyes smoldering, her braids hanging like thick straw-colored ropes against her gray sweatshirt. She was a taller, more severe version of her nine-year-old cousin, with her straight dark eyebrows and small mouth. She looked much older than her eleven years should have allowed — and far too serious.

She felt her pocket for her lucky stone. Lapis lazuli.

Her father had bought it for her at a gem shop in San Diego. "The same color as your eyes," he had said. It felt cool against the warmth of her hand. She could still remember how happy he'd been when he gave it to her. He tied the handles of the plastic bag around her wrist. She had to work to reach the small satin box inside …

Her heart ached just to think of him. Life had seemed so good when he was around. Even her mom was happy then. How she wished he would appear at the bedroom door right now, his laughter filling the room, picking her up and carrying her away from here — away from everything about this terrible life with her awful cousin and this dull little farm in Prince Edward County.

But he was gone now. Gone forever and never coming back. She tried to imagine his face behind the wheel of his car. Did he think of her as the glass shattered all around, the tires screeching, metal twisting? Did he know how lonely she was, now that he was gone? She could feel the tears coming — the tears that she could never control — welling up and spilling over, warm and salty, against her hot cheeks. She lowered her head so Cassel wouldn't see her crying — just one more thing to be ashamed of.

Uncle Norman had tried to help at first. He took her to the school and introduced her around, the silent suspicion of the other kids just making her feel even lonelier. "Teacher's pet," they started calling her behind her back, convinced her good marks were a result of Uncle Norman's influence as a teacher at the school. So she started to let things slip. Stopped studying for tests. Stopped reading the books and doing her homework. Her mother said nothing when she saw the bad reports, her silence more unbearable than any lecture could have been. But what could her mother possibly know about the cruelty of the other kids in grade six?

And then there was the bus. How she hated the bus. Uncle Norman insisted that Cassel sit with her — which she begrudgingly did — only to spend the entire time twisted around in her seat talking to everyone else, and then abandoning her for "real" friends as soon as they reached the school. Cassel would run with her gang of girls to the elementary schoolyard, leaving Wesley alone to fend for herself on the unfriendly middle-school grounds.

Uncle Norman even suggested having lunch with her, but Wesley flatly refused, choosing instead to spend her time in the girl's washroom, locked in one of the stalls, squatting with her feet up on the seat of the toilet so no one would know she was there, eating her lunch alone and waiting for the school bell to ring.

So Uncle Norman gave her the chicks. Twelve of them — a chick for each of her eleven years, plus one "for good measure." He brought them home in a box one day, their fuzzy yellow necks craning as they cheeped with curiosity and fear, their small, scaled feet scratching softly against the cardboard …

Wesley moved the stone through her fingers, glancing furtively at Cassel who was scraping at the frost on the window with her nails. It was so cold outside. Wesley wondered if her chickens would be all right on such a cold night. It never got this cold in California. But this was Picton — a snowy little spot on the north shore of Lake Ontario — all but abandoned in the winter, like every other summer vacation town. And here she was: a stranger in somebody else's bedroom.

In California she had had a big room all to herself with neat shelves displaying her spaceship models and puzzles and books. Now most of her things were in boxes in the basement of her aunt's house, and it was Cassel's drawings of dogs and things that occupied most of the wall space.

There was a terrible fight the first week when she had tried to hang a picture on Cassel's side of the room. It was a photograph of a Lippizaner mare and foal that her father had taken in Austria. Cassel pulled it down from the wall in a territorial rage, the glass shattering in thousands of tiny pieces across the floor. The screaming and crying brought both their mothers into the room. Wesley was inconsolable for days.

Now she had nothing to call her own, except her small flock of chickens. Uncle Norman built her the little shed near the barn to house them — something to keep her occupied after the accident.

"I don't want chickens!" she had screamed. "I want Dad back!"

But that seemed so long ago. Now she poured all her maternal instincts into her "biddies" — keeping their pen clean, fixing the fencing around the shed, and even checking on them late at night with a flashlight, just to see them comfortable and safe on their nests, their startled yellow eyes reflected in the light. Would the shed keep them warm enough tonight? She imagined them inside their coop, heads nestled within their feathers, thin, clawed feet tucked beneath warm breasts.

Wesley looked up to see Cassel staring back at her. She wiped her face quickly with the sleeve of her sweatshirt, preparing for another attack.

But Cassel said nothing. Instead, she reached into the pocket of her overalls and produced a piece of gum, carefully breaking it into two neat pieces. "Bubblegum truce," she whispered, grinning, holding up the gum.

Wesley stared at her cousin for a moment. She didn't want to be nice. She wanted to feel angry and say angry things.

But the feeling never stayed for long. It ebbed and subsided, rolling back to somewhere deep inside her, leaving only the long and empty stretch of loneliness in her heart. She sighed resignedly. "Bubblegum truce," she finally conceded, holding out her pinkie.

Cassel leapt across the room and handed Wesley the gum. The cousins locked pinkies, then crammed the powdery pink gum into their mouths.

"Come on, Wesley," Cassel said, as though nothing had happened. "Let's go see if Mom will forgive us now. We've just *got* to see Holly whelp her puppies." She grabbed Wesley's shirtsleeve, pulling her toward the door. "Besides, you've never seen a bitch whelp before," she added knowingly.

It was so easy for her, Wesley thought. Just like that — a pinkie and a piece of gum — and everything was fine again ...

The girls cautiously opened the door and slunk down the hall. They crept down the stairs, looking through the banister into the living room where Wesley's mother sat sewing by the light of a faded silk floor lamp. Her long black hair hung in a thick plait down her back. She seemed so small, somehow, sitting there by herself.

Wesley watched her mother sew, her deft fingers moving quickly, the silver needle tracing an even rhythm in the fabric. She knew things had been hard for her, too. After ten years at home she was suddenly forced to find a job. She took a computer course at night and managed to get a part-time position as a secretary at a real estate office in town. But the money was barely enough to keep Wesley in shoes, she was growing so fast ...

Rosemary's fingers moved tirelessly. She looked up occasionally to rest her eyes.

"You'll go blind sewing in that light," Aunt Cindy said.

Rosemary stared silently for a moment then gave a long sigh, folding her work in her lap. "It relieves tension," she said at last.

Aunt Cindy placed a sympathetic hand on her sister's shoulder.

"So much fuss over a silly old towel," Rosemary mused sadly.

"It's the age. Dogs do the same thing when they're testing their territory. Every little thing sends them screaming and hollering like it was the end of the world."

Rosemary nodded faintly, looking absently at the work in her lap. "Yes, I suppose."

There was a long, heavy silence.

"You can't blame yourself, Rose," Aunt Cindy finally said. "It isn't your fault. You can't make everything better just by trying harder …"

"Mom," Wesley ventured timidly, ashamed for listening so long.

Aunt Cindy looked angrily over at the girls. "I told you kids to stay in your room."

"We just wanted to know how things were going with Holly … if any pups were here yet," Wesley said.

"We won't fight any more," Cassel chimed in, her normally impudent face glowing with contrived innocence.

Aunt Cindy stood with her arms folded across her chest.

"Isn't it okay now, Cindy?" Rosemary petitioned. "They've promised to be good."

"I've heard that one before," Aunt Cindy scoffed. She stared hard at the girls for a moment, then softened. "Okay, fine. But any more ruckus and it's back to bed. Australian Shepherds are sensitive enough without you kids messing things up. If you make too much noise, you'll upset the mother and she won't have her puppies — or worse," she added pointedly, "she could hurt them."

"Hurt her puppies!" Wesley gasped. The thought of Holly hurting her puppies was a sobering image.

"We'll be good, Mom. I promise," Cassel solemnly pledged, crossing her heart with one finger. "Quiet as little mice." She put her hands up to her face, squeaking like a mouse until Aunt Cindy couldn't help but laugh. Cassel gave Wesley a quick wink, then grabbed her by the hand. "Come on."

» «

Holly was set up in the spare bedroom that doubled as Aunt Cindy's office. On the walls were rows of brightly colored ribbons, hanging from lengths of string. On several pine shelves in the corner, there were trophies of various sizes, some with little statues of dogs and sheep. There was a small desk in one corner, and a neatly made bed with a worn blue and white patchwork quilt against the far wall.

Inside the bedroom, Holly panted heavily. She paced nervously in the whelping pen. Her swollen belly made her movements awkward and slow. The children sat quietly on the bed.

"I bet the first one is gonna be a blue merle, just like Holly," Cassel whispered.

Holly looked up at the sound of her name, her blue and brown marbled eyes glowing in the light by the bed. How funny her mottled coat had looked the first time Wesley had seen it — all dappled with black and gray and white. Blue merle — that's what they called it.

It seemed so confusing at first—all the possibilities. Endless variations on two simple themes of black and red. Aunt Cindy had explained it one day in the barn as they walked along the length of the kennels, the dogs' eager faces shining in the faint light — *blue merle, red merle, black tri, red tri, black bi, red bi, solid black, solid red.* It was the red merle that Wesley liked the most: a soft dappling of red and copper and white, all mottled together like an impressionist painting she had once seen in an art gallery back home.

And their eyes were different from other dogs, too: some mottled in color, like their fur; some crystal clear and blue; some with one brown eye and one blue, the

blue often mistaken for blind by those who didn't know the breed.

"I hope their eyes are crystal blue," Wesley spoke at last, breaking the spell of the silence.

"I like when they're different colors," Cassel mused.

Holly shifted in the pen, moving in slow, deliberate circles. She whined softly, her tongue curling as she panted.

"It's just like waiting for Christmas," Wesley said in a low voice, mesmerized by Holly's strange movements.

"It's better than waiting for Christmas, Wes," Cassel said, glowing, " 'cause when we wake up tomorrow, there'll be little tiny pups squirmin' and snufflin' around." She closed her eyes and scrunched up her face like a puppy searching for its mother.

Wesley laughed softly. It was hard to feel angry when Cassel was being nice, even if she was a pest most of the time.

"How's the young mother?" Uncle Norman asked, walking into the room. He was wearing coveralls, dappled in their own way with small blobs of brightly colored paint. He put his hand on Wesley's shoulder. She didn't turn around, but sat staring at Holly.

"She ain't had any yet, Dad," Cassel answered impudently. "You can see that for yourself."

"Hasn't had any yet," Uncle Norman corrected

her. He tugged on his daughter's braids.

Cassel swiped playfully at his hand.

Uncle Norman reached to tug on Wesley's braids, too, but she jerked her head away. That was *their* father and daughter game. She didn't want any part of it.

Cassel jumped onto the bed, laughing devilishly and swatting at her father's hands.

"Don't start again, Cassel," Aunt Cindy admonished as she appeared in the doorway, her arms burdened with a large cardboard box. On top of the box were some newspapers, the old red towel that had caused so much anguish, and a blanket. "Why don't you quit clowning around and help me for a change?"

Cassel bunny-hopped across the bed. She reached for the towel and newspapers, placing them on the floor next to the pen.

Aunt Cindy turned to her husband. "What are you going to do?"

"Well … it's late, and I've got to go to school tomorrow — even if these kids think they can play hooky over a litter of pups." He winked at his daughter.

"Well, you know the rule, Dad," Cassel piped up. "Help out or clear out!"

"Right, boss!" he said, laughing. He turned and gave a mock salute to Aunt Cindy, then marched out of the room.

It was late for a school night, and Uncle Norman would have to get up early for his morning class, but

Wesley knew he wouldn't go to bed right away. He would sneak off again and work on one of his paintings in the dim light and damp of the basement, the way he did every night after the rest of the house had gone to sleep.

Holly continued to pace, stopping suddenly to snap furiously at her sides. She whined softly, her breath quick and shallow. She started to dig mechanically, her instinct to build a den thwarted by the wooden floor of the whelping pen.

Aunt Cindy knelt down beside the pen. She unfolded the newspapers, carefully covering the floor. She opened the box and pulled out a heat lamp and a small white scale for weighing the puppies. Then she produced some cotton swabs, a bottle of iodine and a shiny little pair of scissors. She folded the blanket and placed it in the box. She clamped the heat lamp to the side of the whelping pen, adjusting the height over the cardboard box so that it wouldn't throw off too much heat.

Rosemary appeared carrying a small lacquered wooden tray with four cups of tea. She handed the cups solemnly to Aunt Cindy and the girls, took one for herself, then sat down on the bed to wait. "Radio says a big storm's coming," she said.

Holly whined, then tried to lie down, only to groan to her feet again and continue to pace. It was going to be a long night.

## 2.

## THE SNOW COMES

The snow came in the night, falling steadily on the little farm. Inside the barn, the sheep shifted restlessly in their pen, their muffled bleats curling steam into the air. In the kennels, the dogs lay in tight, indiscernible balls beneath their heating lamps, the narrow orange cones of light a welcome defense against the cold. Outside, a frosty wind shivered over the ground, lifting swirls of glittering snow through the skirts of the dark pines that leaned toward the warmth of the house.

The girls pressed their faces against the window in the living room. They had long since been banned from the room where Holly still panted and whined, awaiting the arrival of her puppies.

"Too many people," Aunt Cindy had said.

The television droned in the background, barely audible over the wind outside. Images of abandoned cars and frozen buildings flashed across the screen. The stained-glass window at the front of the living room rattled violently in its frame. It showed an Australian Shepherd chasing a small flock of sheep, with Aunt Cindy's kennel name, *Triblue*, in meticulous cerulean glass letters underneath. It looked so fragile, as though the wind would punch the shapes from their lead work, the glass shattering in a kaleidoscope of color on the floor.

At last the bedroom door opened. Rosemary appeared looking tired and serious. The children rushed over to meet her.

"Are they here yet?" Cassel asked.

Rosemary shook her head. "We're still in the dark, kids," she said wearily. She smiled, trying to make light of the situation.

"Is something wrong with Holly, Mom?" Wesley asked gravely.

Rosemary put her arms around the two girls. She spoke softly, as though giving voice to her own troubled thoughts. "She's ready to have her puppies, but so far she hasn't had any yet. We aren't sure why. Aunt Cindy is going to call the vet to hear what she has to say. We may have to take Holly to the clinic, although I don't see how that will be possible with this storm going on."

"The whole world is frozen, Auntie Rose!" Cassel blurted out. "The snow has been falling for hours. The cars and trucks are piled up all over the place. We saw it on TV! The snowplows can't keep up with the snow and people can't get home to their families. It's the biggest, iciest, snowiest storm I've ever seen in my life!"

Rosemary laughed. Cassel's excitement was welcome relief from the worries of the evening.

But Wesley was not so easily distracted. What if something *was* wrong with Holly — something terrible? She bit her nails nervously, her eyes unfocused and staring out the window at the storm. She imagined the wind and snow on the lake, the normally calm surface churning, the waves curling and frothing as they crashed against the shore. She imagined the sand on the great dunes down in West Lake, blowing in seamless bronze sheets out to the water ...

Aunt Cindy emerged from the bedroom.

"Can we see Holly, Mom?" Cassel asked.

Aunt Cindy glowered. "Only if you are quiet," she said with irritation. "No loud voices or horsing around."

The girls nodded silently, then moved into the bedroom, their faces as somber as though they were going to church.

Aunt Cindy shuffled into the kitchen. She flipped through a small worn address book until she found the veterinarian's phone number, then dialed, waiting absently for the answering service to pick up the line. She would have to leave a message. No one would be at the clinic this late at night. She prayed that Dr. Voight would call her back soon.

The phone rang and rang. Aunt Cindy grew discouraged. Perhaps the storm was responsible...

Suddenly, the phone was picked up, only to be dropped and picked up again. The line crackled and buzzed. A small, breathless voice answered through the storm.

"Dr. Voight here!"

"Dr. Voight!" Aunt Cindy exclaimed with surprise.

"Yes. What do you want?!" the doctor's thin voice strained through the static like she was transmitting through a cheap radio.

"It's Cindy Graham. I'm a bit surprised to hear your voice. I expected the answering service."

"What? I can't hear you!" the doctor yelled.

The storm raged through the phone line.

"I expected the answering service!" Aunt Cindy shouted into the phone.

"Who? What do you want?" the doctor's thin voice demanded.

"It's Cindy Graham. I'm calling about Holly."

The line popped and buzzed.

"I came in on an emergency," the doctor's small voice explained. "Blasted snow froze me in. What can I ...?" Her voice faded in and out of the crackle.

"Well ... it's ... *Holly*," Aunt Cindy stammered. "She's having some trouble. It's her first litter and all, and I just wondered if ..."

"Have you felt her abdomen? Have the puppies dropped?"

"Yes, I think so ..."

"Well there's nothing I can do from here. You'd have to bring her in. And I don't see how you're going to do that with this storm."

"Yes, I know. I just thought maybe —"

"Well you know as well as I do that it could just be —" The phone popped and fell silent.

Aunt Cindy stared at the phone in frustration and disbelief. "I've been cut off!" She clicked the receiver several times, but the line was dead. She slammed the phone angrily into its cradle.

The lights flickered as though in warning, then went out at all once, leaving the house in total blackness. "Oh, for Pete's sake," Aunt Cindy cussed. She could hear the girls shouting with surprise from the bedroom. "Light the candle next to the bed!" she yelled out. She felt blindly along the counter, then pulled one of the drawers open. She rummaged around, grabbed a small flashlight and clicked it on with a snap. The soft beam barely illuminated the drawer. She dug out a handful of candles and a box of matches, then made her way with the flashlight through the dark.

Just then, Rosemary yelled from the bedroom. "I think something's happening!"

# 3.

## TRAGEDY

Aunt Cindy rushed into the bed-room. Rosemary and the girls were crowded around the whelp-ing pen in what seemed to be a strange ritual. Between cupped hands, Rosemary sheltered the flame of a short white candle, the flickering glow sending eerie shadows dancing across the room. "I saw something just before the lights went out," she said. She spoke in a hushed voice, as though the uncertain light of the candle demanded it.

Aunt Cindy set more candles around the room, lighting them as she went. The flames leapt and gut-tered in the draft from the window. "It's not great, but it will have to do," she said as she lit the last candle.

Holly was hunched over in the whelping pen, her

eyes glazed, her sides heaving as she panted. Aunt Cindy squatted down next to the pen. She watched Holly in silence for some time, as though in a trance. Holly turned around and around in the pen. A dark form suddenly emerged, then disappeared again.

"There it is!" Rosemary whispered excitedly.

Aunt Cindy nodded knowingly. "It's big and it's breech. Poor girl. No wonder she's been having so much trouble."

"What's *breech*, Mom?" Wesley asked.

"Backwards — feet first instead of head first," Rosemary murmured, her eyes trained on the panting dog. "Is there anything we can do to help her?"

"Not really," Aunt Cindy said. "We have to wait and hope for the best at this point. If she whelps this one soon, the others shouldn't cause much trouble."

Holly tried to sit down but jumped up again with a yelp. She whined loudly, her body contracted violently, and a very large puppy popped out into the pen. Wesley gasped. Holly spun around and looked at the dark wet form. She licked it a few times, then bit the placenta to free the puppy. She licked the puppy over and over, until Aunt Cindy reached in and gently picked it up.

By the light of the candles, Aunt Cindy carefully cut the umbilical cord and swabbed it with iodine. Then she rubbed the puppy with the red towel and placed it on the scale. "Born at 12:04 A.M. Nine and a half ounces," she announced excitedly. She scribbled the information into a small black notebook. "And it's a girl," she said proudly, holding the puppy up. "A blue merle with a natural bobtail. She's beautiful."

"I told you the first one was gonna be a blue merle!" Cassel said, beaming.

Holly looked nervously at Aunt Cindy. She wanted her puppy back.

"It's okay, girl," Aunt Cindy reassured the new mother, "I'll give her back." She gave the puppy another quick inspection, then carefully placed it in the pen.

The puppy looked like a guinea pig with its blunt little nose and skinny little legs. Its eyes were closed and it squirmed slowly, trying to find its mother. Holly snuffed and nosed the puppy toward her swollen teats, but before it could nurse, she whined and groaned to her feet.

"There's another one coming already!" Aunt Cindy exclaimed, reaching in and taking the first puppy. "I don't want her to step on this little one in the process." She placed the puppy in the box with the blanket. She leaned over to snap on the heating lamp then caught herself, realizing the electricity was off.

Holly looked anxiously toward the box, but the pain of labor shifted her focus to the next arrival.

"They're probably waiting in line after all this time," Rosemary quietly joked.

Holly moved around in the pen. Her body contracted suddenly, and another puppy was born.

Aunt Cindy squinted at the puppy. "It's a red merle," she whispered. "And it has a natural bobtail, too."

Holly licked and licked the puppy. She snuffed and prodded it with her nose but the puppy did not move. Aunt Cindy leaned over and gently picked it up. "I think it's dead."

"Oh no!" Rosemary cried. "Why?"

Aunt Cindy inspected the puppy for a moment. "Its oxygen was probably cut off. Must have been God's will, though. Look ..." She held out her hands. The dead puppy lay small and wet in the candle light. "It's a runt."

"How can you be so cruel?!" Wesley suddenly screamed. "How can you just stand there and talk like that?! Why don't you do something! Why don't you help the poor little thing!"

Aunt Cindy stood in shock, staring at her niece.

"That's the way you treat everything!" Wesley shouted. "It's so unfair! I can't stand it!" She burst into hysterical tears, throwing herself on the bed.

Rosemary clumped the candle onto the night table and rushed to her daughter's side. Cassel covered her face and began to wail. Aunt Cindy lunged for the old red towel, wrapping the tiny puppy inside. She began vigorously rubbing the pup, stopping occasionally to blow into its small, damp nose. Holly whined softly as Aunt Cindy opened the towel. The puppy did not move.

"You have to help it," Wesley sobbed. "Don't let the little thing die!"

Aunt Cindy folded the towel and rubbed even faster than before. She looked at the puppy again, blew into its nose and continued to rub.

After an eternity of rubbing and blowing, Aunt Cindy opened the towel and peeked inside. Everyone froze in anticipation. Wesley let out an involuntary sob from the bed. How could the innocent little thing die before its life had even started? They all stared at the tiny puppy in Aunt Cindy's hands, the candles sputtering as the wind from the storm roared against the window. The puppy lay damp and lifeless, then slowly squirmed its head and feet.

"It's alive!" Wesley cried. "You did it, Aunt Cindy! You did it!" She buried her face in a pillow, her body wracked with sobs of relief.

Cassel began to wail again. Rosemary anxiously rubbed her daughter's back. Aunt Cindy stood staring at her niece in confused silence. She should have warned her that something like this could happen. She placed the puppy on the scale. It was a female as well, but much smaller than the first one, weighing only six and a half ounces. Runt, she thought disdainfully. She gingerly placed both puppies in the pen with Holly who sat panting and waiting expectantly. Holly sniffed the puppies as she lay down, curling tightly around them. She was exhausted.

# 4.

## FOUR MORE

 The lights flared on with a surge, the sound of the TV suddenly hissing from the living room. Aunt Cindy scowled at the girls sitting on the bed, their faces red with worry and excitement. "You kids go to bed," she ordered tiredly. "This is difficult enough without having to deal with all your screaming and crying. That runt wasn't meant for this world. If it had been up to me, I would have let it go."

Wesley's face crumpled in shame.

"I can't sell it for more than a pet — if it even makes it that far! It could be brain damaged, for all we know, and have to be euthanized. What are folks gonna think when I start breeding dogs like that? It'll be the end of my reputation, I can tell you that for sure."

The girls sat silently on the bed.

"It's my fault, really," Rosemary spoke. "I should have known that something like this could happen. It all seemed so innocent — watching the puppies." She twisted her hands in her lap. "I don't know much about these things … but can one tiny puppy really cause so much harm?"

Aunt Cindy stood with her arms folded, her lips tightly pursed. She looked over at Holly who was curled happily around her two puppies. She slowly knelt down and methodically changed the newspapers on the floor, crumpling the dirty ones into a green garbage bag. "Any more outbursts and you kids are out," she finally said.

Rosemary sighed softly with relief. The cousins nodded solemnly, moving closer to get a better look at the pups. Together they watched the puppies in amazed silence. Aunt Cindy left the room, clicked the TV off, then returned. She moved through the room, carefully blowing out the candles.

"What if she turns out okay?" Wesley tentatively asked.

"Who?" Aunt Cindy demanded gruffly.

"The red merle," Wesley said, almost in a whisper.

Aunt Cindy turned in disbelief to where her niece sat on the bed. "I don't keep pets on this farm, Wesley, you know that. What do I want with that runt?"

"You said you wanted to keep some pups from this

litter — if they turned out."

"I need good strong dogs, Wesley," Aunt Cindy explained. "For herding, and to pass on the bloodlines."

"But what if the red merle turns out? Can we keep her then?" Wesley's tear-stained face stared back in earnest.

Aunt Cindy looked away. The world is hard and cruel sometimes, she thought. "That runt won't amount to much," she muttered.

"I can help take care of her," Wesley bravely continued. "I'll take responsibility. Help feed her and train her and things. I can even help pay for the food. I've got my savings in the bank."

"I think we should keep her, Mom" Cassel joined in.

Aunt Cindy turned angrily to her daughter. "You know I don't keep pets, Cassel!" she snapped. "These dogs are my business — *our* business. They have to work — or go. The same rule applies to the little red merle!"

"But couldn't you just give her a chance?" Wesley implored. "How will you know unless you give her a chance?"

Her aunt scrubbed at her hair in frustration. She looked at the little red merle lying in the pen. The pup's markings were bold, with a big patch of red around each eye and several more on her back and legs. Her feet were pure white and her coat was peppered with copper flashes. She is pretty, even if she doesn't have a good start on things, Aunt Cindy thought.

But pretty doesn't count for much in the field. And it was hard enough for a strong, healthy dog to make it. How would Wesley feel if they had to get rid of the dog later on, after she had grown attached to it? "I won't give that runt special consideration," she said. "She'll get the same chance as any of the others."

"But you will give her a chance, right?" Wesley persisted. "You won't just sell her right away — as a pet?"

"Sure, yeah," Aunt Cindy conceded with a wave. "But I'm not making any promises."

Wesley jumped from the bed, throwing her arms around her aunt. "You won't regret it, Aunt Cindy. I swear."

"Okay, okay," her aunt grumbled, peeling Wesley's arms from her waist. "Now let me be, for heaven's sake. We have work to do!"

As though listening, Holly groaned to her feet. She sniffed the puppies and began to pace around the pen.

"Right on cue," Aunt Cindy said, grabbing the two pups and placing them in the heated box.

For the next three hours, Holly panted and pushed, bringing four more puppies into the world. The girls watched with quiet wonder as Aunt Cindy cleaned and weighed the new arrivals. They were all boys, and three of them were black tricolored. The last one was a blue merle, just like Holly. His markings were soft and muddled except for his face with a black patch over the left eye.

Outside, the storm raged on as Aunt Cindy tended to the last puppy. The snow swirled against the bedroom window, collecting in little drifts in the corners to create a small circular opening, like a porthole, into the eye of the storm. The girls, who had faithfully stayed awake until the final puppy arrived, drifted happily off to sleep on the bed.

"Poor little things," Rosemary whispered as she covered them with the worn blue and white quilt. "I'm sure they thought that something would go wrong if they didn't stay awake."

Aunt Cindy managed a smile from her seat on the floor. Holly had done amazingly well for her first litter, despite all the confusion. She watched the young mother gently nuzzle the squirming pups. Six puppies was a good size for a first litter. I hope there's a winner in there, she thought. As for the fate of the little red merle — only time will tell.

"How about a cup of tea?" Rosemary asked, breaking her sister's reverie. "I already have the kettle on."

Aunt Cindy nodded.

The phone jangled loudly from the kitchen. Rosemary ran to answer it before the ringing woke the girls.

"Who would be calling at this time of night?" Aunt Cindy asked with irritation.

"It's Dr. Voight!" Rosemary announced from the doorway.

Aunt Cindy groaned to her feet and trotted softly

out of the room. She carefully explained Holly's experience to the vet, repeating herself several times when the storm and the kettle interfered with the call. She promised to call Dr. Voight in the morning and then hung up the phone. "It seems like she's going to be there all night," she reported to Rosemary who was already hunched over a steaming mug of tea at the kitchen table.

"Is she out there alone?" Rosemary asked with concern.

"I guess so. I think she has some blankets and coffee." Aunt Cindy rubbed her forehead in exhaustion, then drew the blind open on the window by the door. The cold had decorated the glass with a frosty lace curtain. "I can't see a thing!" she exclaimed. She scraped at the frost with her nails, then tried to open the door. The wood cracked and creaked in protest, refusing to open. "I think we're actually snowed in!"

"I can't remember a winter like this before," Rosemary mused.

"You were spoiled, living in California."

Rosemary nodded. "Yeah …," she said wistfully.

The women fell silent. They sipped quietly at their tea while the wind howled and moaned outside. Despite the hour and the worries of the night, it was some time before they shuffled off to bed.

» «

The lonely cries of the coyotes mingled with the wind in the night. Inside the whelping pen, Holly curled tightly around her little pups. She sighed with satisfaction and closed her eyes. She would stir several times in the night to feed the puppies and to lick their fur, but for now she slept.

# 5.

## THE SURPRISE

 The girls woke to the soft whimpers of the pups struggling to find the warmth of their mother and her nourishing milk. Holly had left the pen to stretch her legs and drink some water. The sound of the puppies crying sent her trotting back to the pen.

"Would you look at that!" Cassel exclaimed with wonder from her perch on the side of the bed. "Look at them go."

Wesley hugged her knees and watched the puppies in silence. Last night seemed like a long and distant dream. She couldn't believe that the puppies had finally arrived. "Look at the little red one," she said, pointing to the red merle. "It's hard to believe that she almost didn't make it."

"She's a miracle," Cassel said with hushed awe.

"She is a miracle," Wesley agreed, her arms still folded around her knees. But suddenly she sprang off the bed as though stung by a bee. "Who's that?" she asked excitedly, pointing to the puppies.

Cassel jumped off the bed. "Who's who?"

"Who's that puppy? That little black tri with the white feet! It wasn't there last night!"

Cassel leaned over the pen and did a quick count of the puppies. "One, two, three, four, five, six … *seven!* You're right, Wes! There's seven!"

"Holly must have had another one while we were sleeping!" Wesley exclaimed.

"Good girl, Holly," Cassel praised, stroking the dog on the head. "You're a good mother to your babies."

Aunt Cindy appeared at the door. "Have you looked outside yet? The storm seems to be over."

"Mom!" Cassel shrieked. "You won't believe this! Holly had another puppy in the night!"

Aunt Cindy rushed over to the pen.

"See!" Wesley shouted. "It's the little black one with the white feet. It wasn't here last night!"

Her aunt stared down at the puppy. "Well, would you look at that! She must have had it while we were all lying back and relaxing." She reached in and picked up the puppy. "Another little black tri male." She looked it over admiringly, then placed it on the scale. "Ten and a half ounces." She scribbled in the little record book. "Good girl, Holly," she said, placing the puppy back in the pen with the others.

Holly stood up to acknowledge the praise, sending the pups tumbling from her teats to the floor of the pen. Aunt Cindy stroked her head for a moment, lavishing her with attention, then told her to lie down again so that the puppies could nurse. The little red merle was the first to find a nipple and began nursing greedily, her tiny paws massaging and pushing at Holly's side.

"Look at the little red merle!" Cassel exclaimed. "She's really something!"

"Have you thought of any names yet?" Aunt Cindy asked.

"I thought of one for the little red merle," Wesley said hopefully, pulling a worn piece of paper from her pocket and unfolding it. It was a pedigree, written in pencil, in neat, small letters. She cleared her throat softly, then began. "Her sire's name is Cadillac Jack. He's out of Motown Slick and Lena." She pushed her hair behind her ears, then continued. "Holly's registered name is Wind Chimes."

"She's a *double* champion," Cassel added excitedly.

Wesley nodded in agreement. "Holly's out of Still Crazy and Dancing In The Dark. Now everybody knows Jack. He's famous in the United States *and* Canada. I thought we should name the little red merle after her sire."

"Boy! You've really done your homework!" Aunt

Cindy said, impressed with her niece's diligence. "What did you have in mind?"

"Well …," Wesley hesitated.

"She wants to name her Spitfire, like the model airplane her dad kept in his office!" Cassel burst out.

"A Spitfire is a type of car," Wesley explained, "so it fits with Cadillac Jack. And it's a plane, too … so it reminds me of my dad." She looked wistfully down at the paper.

"Tell my mom the rest," Cassel said, pointing furiously to the pedigree. "Read what it means, Wes."

Wesley cleared her throat again, holding the paper at arm's length. "Spitfire: 1) a British-built fighter engaged in every major action flown by the Royal Air Force between 1939 and 1945. A symbol of victory against overwhelming odds and the only fighter to achieve legendary status; 2) a person given to outbursts of spiteful temper and anger, especially a woman."

"We looked it up in the dictionary!" Cassel said, beaming.

Aunt Cindy frowned thoughtfully. "Triblue's Spitfire." She tested the name on her tongue. "It's a good name. I hope that runt can live up to it. But what about her call name, her everyday name?"

"I thought we could call her Piper," Wesley said. "Her grandpa's name is Drum, and her mom's name is Wind Chimes. They're both musical names, so I thought Piper would be good. And a Piper is a plane too, so it matches with her registered name." Wesley looked up at her aunt for approval.

Aunt Cindy shook her head in quiet defeat.

"*I* think it's a good name," Cassel proclaimed, staring at the puppy. "It's like she's spitting mad and nothing is going to stop her."

Wesley moved over to the pen to look at the puppy more closely. "Triblue's Spitfire," she said softly, reaching in to stroke the squirming little form. The puppy squeaked and jerked away from its mother. "I think she likes it!" Wesley said, laughing at the puppy's clumsy movements. She picked the puppy up, holding it to the light. "What do you think of that, Piper? What do you think of your name?"

Piper squirmed helplessly, grunting in vain protest, her tiny eyes closed. Holly jumped to her feet, sending the other pups tumbling once again to the floor of the pen. She whined softly, watching Wesley and the puppy.

"It's time for Holly to go outside," Aunt Cindy said. She clucked softly, trying to coax Holly out of the pen, but the dog would not come. She tried offering her a piece of food. Holly stared absently. She tried clapping and running toward the door. No response. Holly was not ready to leave her puppies behind, and she certainly wasn't going to leave while Wesley was holding Piper.

Finally, after much fruitless cajoling and coaxing,

Aunt Cindy was forced to snap a collar and leash on the reluctant dog to encourage her out of the pen. Holly looked anxiously back at her puppies before finally conceding to walk outside.

Once out in the snow, Holly seemed to come to life, barking loudly when Aunt Cindy bent down to make a snowball. But even the crisp winter landscape could not occupy her interest for long. She wanted to return to her little pups. She pulled on the leash, looking expectantly from her owner to the door of the house.

When they returned to the bedroom, Aunt Cindy unsnapped the collar and Holly trotted happily to the pen. She quickly inspected her puppies to make sure that everything was in order before curling protectively around them.

"Come on, girls," Aunt Cindy said. "Let's get some breakfast and tell the others about the new pup."

Uncle Norman had already started breakfast when Aunt Cindy and the girls entered the kitchen. The sweet smell of pancakes and maple syrup filtered through the house. Goblin, Cassel's little black and white kitten, was winking from his lookout on top of the old honey cupboard. Hailing from a long line of mousers, Goblin was acquired to rid the house of pests. He proved his worth early on, catching three mice on the first day, and stacking them in a neat pile by the kitchen door.

"Why aren't you at school, Dad?" Cassel asked,

trying to reach the kitten on his roost.

"Why aren't *you* at school?" Uncle Norman answered back.

" 'Cause we helped with the puppies. You know that."

"I'm playing hooky too, then," Uncle Norman said happily, flipping a pancake in the air.

"It's a snow day," Aunt Cindy confirmed. "Did you hear about the big surprise this morning?"

"Don't tell me," Uncle Norman joked, holding his hand to his forehead like a psychic. "Your dog just had puppies!"

"Genius," Aunt Cindy snorted.

"I know!" Rosemary exclaimed, appearing in the doorway. "There's another puppy. I just counted them."

"So how many is that, now?" Uncle Norman asked.

"Seven!" Wesley and Cassel chimed together.

"What's for breakfast?" Aunt Cindy demanded, pounding her fist on the table in mock demand. "I'm starving!"

Uncle Norman produced a tall stack of pancakes from the oven, and placed them in front of his wife with a flourish.

"We're gonna call the red merle Spitfire!" Cassel suddenly announced, brandishing her fork in the air. "And her call name is Piper."

Rosemary looked over at her daughter, who nodded shyly in agreement. Had they done the right thing, saving the puppy? Wesley did look happy this morning for the first time in ages.

As the girls marveled over the morning's surprise, Uncle Norman looked fondly around the table. "Look at you," he said at last. "You look just like a scene from *Little Women.*"

Wesley gazed around the room. Everything looked delicious in the warmth of the small kitchen. It wasn't as though anything had changed, really. The curtains were still the same old muslin cloth, and the tiles on the floor were still dull and scratched and needing to be replaced. But somehow, things looked different today — almost cheerful. The sun seemed to glow from inside the maple syrup jar, the syrup's liquid sweetness pouring honey gold reflections against the white of the tablecloth.

"What's on the agenda for the little women today?" Rosemary asked.

"Chores," Aunt Cindy said.

"Painting," Uncle Norman added.

"Not before chores," Aunt Cindy countered.

"Tobogganing," Uncle Norman said. "That's a chore." He winked at Wesley, who looked away, but not soon enough to hide her smile.

"Why do I bother?" Aunt Cindy sighed with exasperation.

"Because you really, really love me?" Uncle Norman

cooed mockingly, leaning his chin in one hand.

Aunt Cindy rolled her eyes. Rosemary and the girls burst into laughter. If Uncle Norman knew about the little red merle and all the trouble from the night before, he certainly didn't show it.

She's going to work out, Wesley thought to herself. I'll prove it.

The cousins wolfed down their breakfast, then bolted from the table to the spare bedroom. Holly greeted them at the door, walking them back to the pen. The puppies lay sleeping, their bellies swollen after their morning feed. They jerked in little fits as they slept, tiny beads of milk speckling their muzzles.

Holly stepped into the pen and curled possessively around her pups. She nudged them under her belly and covered them with her head. She was not ready to let the children play with her new babies.

"Come on, Wes," Cassel urged. "Let's go play baby with Goblin."

"Not yet," Wesley said, remembering the chickens. "I have to check on the biddies."

» «

When she was finally dressed warmly enough to suit her mother, Wesley grabbed her small silver feed pail from its nail in the mud room and thumped down the stairs into the snow. The storm had transformed the farm into a strange and glittering landscape. The snow stretched everywhere in smooth, pristine drifts, broken only by the dark hoops of maple saplings that breached the glistening surface, their trunks bowed by the wind and ice. Overhead, the power lines and branches of the bigger trees were carefully decorated with long, sharp icicles that glinted in the morning sun. Wesley reached up and broke an icicle from one of the branches and tasted it. It was cold and slightly metallic against her tongue.

"How's the San Francisco Kid?" Mr. Sharp called out from his driveway.

"San Diego, Mr. Sharp," Wesley corrected, waving the icicle in greeting. "I lived in San Diego — not San Francisco."

Mr. Sharp just nodded, grunting as he strained to lift a heavy scoop of snow.

"Should you be doing that?" Wesley asked, pointing the icicle toward the shovel.

"The price of living alone," Mr. Sharp puffed.

"Maybe you should hire someone to help out," Wesley suggested.

Mr. Sharp stopped and leaned on his shovel, pushing his toque to the back of his head. His round face was red and beaded with sweat. "Hire somebody?" he snorted. "Do I look so old to your young eyes?"

"No, Mr. Sharp. Not at all. It's just … it seems like a lot of work for one person. I mean … with your sheep and all. Aunt Cindy can barely take care of the few she's got, and she has Uncle Norman and me and Cassel to help."

"You mean, you girls actually help around the house? I thought you just got in the way and caused trouble." Mr. Sharp winked.

Wesley raised her silver pail in defense. "I take care of the biddies. And I helped out with the puppies, too."

Mr. Sharp nodded his head in amusement. "I heard all about it from your uncle this morning. Heard you got yourself a little pup, too."

Wesley licked the icicle thoughtfully. "We're not sure yet. We have to wait and see if she works out." She pushed the hair from her eyes. "I'm going to train her," she added hopefully.

Mr. Sharp raised his eyebrows in surprise then dug his shovel into the snow. "That's a lot of work."

Wesley nodded. She waited for Mr. Sharp to speak again, but he just puffed and groaned and shoveled. "Well ... got to feed the biddies," she finally said, waving the silver pail.

She turned and shuffled through the snow to the barn, thinking about Mr. Sharp. His wife was gone and his kids were long since grown. And he never saw his grandchildren much, it seemed. Was he lonely in that big farmhouse by himself?

Wesley liked Mr. Sharp. He was always friendly — although he might not be if he knew how she liked to sneak up to the loft in his barn. She would go there to think about things — things she couldn't tell anyone else. Like boys, for instance. Would she ever have a boyfriend? Or would she be alone for the rest of her life, like Mr. Sharp — and now her mother?

There wasn't anyone special at school, yet. Oh, there were some nice boys, like Dennis Mitchell and Stephen Reynolds, but they had girls already. And there was Kyle Anderson, but he was in grade eight. He was a great hockey player — that's what everybody said. He had actually talked to her once or twice while they waited to catch the bus home at the end of the day. His dad bred Border Collies and he had held the national title five years in a row. Aunt Cindy wasn't keen on Kyle's dad. She called him "Border Collie folk." But Kyle was so friendly and cute, and all the girls liked him. She'd heard them talking in the bathroom at recess ...

Wesley stopped on a small hill in the path, turning around to look back toward the house. Through the kitchen window of the house, she could see Aunt Cindy and her mom bustling about the kitchen. Uncle Norman stood at the sink, up to his elbows in dishwater. Cassel balanced on tiptoe, attempting to retrieve the kitten from the honey cupboard. The rows of dishes stood on shelves behind glass doors above the stove. A straw wreath, twined with ribbon from several Christmases before, decorated the far wall.

It was a serene, domestic scene, the kind Wesley used to admire in the Italian sugar eggs at Easter when she was little. She wondered what it would be like to see her father there, warm and laughing at the table, his big hands gesticulating as he told one of his stories. She imagined herself there, too, sitting next to him, her blue eyes upturned and shining toward his gentle, loving face.

Wesley stood in the snow, her coat open, the little silver pail dangling from one hand. She looked through the window for a while, then turned away, trudging down the path to the coop.

She stepped carefully over the chicken wire into the pen. The feedbox leaned against the small barn-board chicken coop. On the ground all around the pen there were tiny white feathers in the snow. Wesley could hear the chickens softly clucking inside. She opened the feedbox, scooping grain into the pail. Bending down, so as not to catch her jacket on the small door, she stuck her head inside the coop. "How are the biddies?" she asked in a low voice.

The hens squawked and clucked in greeting, rushing past her legs into the pen. Wesley scattered the grain on the snow for the hungry chickens, talking quietly to them as they pecked and scratched the ground. When the pail was empty, Wesley crawled into the coop to inspect the nests. There were eggs in three of them. She carefully transferred the smooth, warm forms to the pockets of her jacket.

When Wesley returned to the warmth of the kitchen, the discussion had turned to tail dockings and vaccinations. She took the eggs out of her pockets, placing them gently in the little slots on the door inside the refrigerator.

Cassel was waiting impatiently, holding Goblin wrapped in an old afghan. "Come on, Wes," she said. "The baby is hungry and he needs his diaper changed."

The girls rushed into the ironing room, closing the door behind them. They built a bed from pillows and blankets, then dressed the reluctant kitten in old baby clothes. They played this game for hours, until Rosemary called them for lunch.

## 6.

## GROWING

 At three days old, the pups had their first visit to Dr. Voight. The children begged to come but Aunt Cindy flatly refused. "It isn't going to be a nice visit. Some of the pups will need their tails docked. They won't like it and they'll cry."

"Why do it, then?" Wesley asked, trying to hide the emotion in her voice.

"Have to," Aunt Cindy answered matter-of-factly. "It's the breed standard. Some pups are born with natural bobtails, some aren't. The ones with tails are sometimes deformed in some way. Kind of twisted and funny looking. Anyway, it's the way it is — like it or not."

Wesley nodded her head. She wanted to be okay

with the whole thing but it wasn't easy. "Will they get their needles, too?"

"Not 'til they're seven weeks old. They get their first vaccinations then. You can come for that if you want."

Holly didn't want to go to the vet. She refused to jump into her crate in the car, so Aunt Cindy picked her up and put her in, adjusting the sheepskin liner on the floor of the crate before closing and locking the cage door. Uncle Norman drove to the clinic, Aunt Cindy in the passenger seat with the pups in a smaller crate on her lap.

When they returned, Wesley and Cassel were waiting at the kitchen door. They did not speak as Aunt Cindy carried the crate of pups to the spare bedroom, Holly trotting anxiously alongside. The pups were carefully returned to the whelping pen. Holly curled around them, snuffing and prodding the squirming forms to her swollen teats. She gave a loud sigh of relief, happy to be back with her babies.

Wesley and Cassel waited patiently on the bed for Aunt Cindy to finish with the puppies. When she left the room, the girls moved in to get a closer look. All of the puppies had bobtails now. Five of them had been docked, the color of iodine still staining their fur like rust. At the ends of their small tails, the sutures stuck out like angry black bristles.

Looking at the dark stitches, Wesley was glad Piper had a natural bob.

Most of the pups were too exhausted to eat, but Piper was feeding greedily, her tiny paws pushing in an instinctive rhythm as she nursed.

"She's taking advantage of the situation," Cassel said, smiling.

Wesley laughed softly, amazed at the puppy's appetite. "She's making up for lost time."

» «

As the days of winter marched on in regular procession, the puppies grew and flourished. There were even one or two that showed some promise, Aunt Cindy said. What made them promising, though, Wesley wasn't quite sure. One was the biggest pup in the litter, but he seemed rather reserved. The other was rambunctious and bold — but not nearly as feisty as Piper. When Wesley pointed out this obvious fact, Aunt Cindy was noncommittal. "It's too early to say how that runt will turn out," she said.

If Piper was the runt of the litter, it certainly hadn't held her back. She was growing rapidly and was the first puppy to open her eyes.

"She's going to be a champion," Wesley cooed, holding the puppy proudly up to the light and gazing into her crystal-clear blue eyes.

"You don't know that," Cassel sneered. "You can't tell just by looking at her. She may not take to the sheep and then she'll have to go. No pets on the farm — that's what Mom always says."

"She will work out!" Wesley snarled at her cousin. "You just wait and see." She buried her face in the puppy's soft, red fur. It was warm and sweet, like the smell of new cedar shavings. She knew Piper didn't have a good chance. She was a runt. She was born dead. She would have to prove herself or go. That's what Aunt Cindy had said.

Piper licked at Wesley's face, her pink tongue rough and warm. Wesley couldn't help but laugh, the puppy nipping and snuffing at her nose. "Please work out," she whispered.

» «

The people who came to see the pups were fascinated by Piper. Even to their untrained eyes they could see that Piper was special. They loved the color of her fur, her crystal blue eyes, her bold personality. They all wanted to pick her up and carry her around. One person even offered to pay more for "the little red one." All this attention made Wesley nervous. "She's not for sale," she asserted, over and over again.

At school, Wesley daydreamed endlessly about Piper, getting reprimanded more than once for her reveries. What if someone offered her aunt so much money she couldn't refuse to sell the little red merle?

What if Aunt Cindy decided to get rid of her anyway? At the end of the day, she would run feverishly down the lane, desperate to see the pup, terrified at what she might find when she got home.

One morning, Wesley woke especially early to check on the puppies. But when she walked into the spare bedroom, the pups were gone! In the corner where the whelping pen had been stood a scrubbed wooden chair with an old crocheted afghan neatly folded over the back.

"Oh no!" Wesley choked. Her eyes blurred with tears as she raced up the stairs. She burst into the bedroom and jumped on Cassel's bed, shaking her sleeping cousin violently by the shoulder. "Cassel! Wake up!"

Cassel swatted sleepily at Wesley's hands, rolling over to face the wall. "Leave me alone," she mumbled.

"You have to get up," Wesley begged. "They're gone!"

Cassel shot up in bed, her face wild with confusion. "Who?!"

"The puppies!" Wesley gasped. "They're all gone. Holly too — the pen — everything!"

Cassel stared at her cousin in shock, then waved her arm dismissively. "They ain't gone, Wesley," she scoffed, rolling up in her covers and facing the wall again. "Mom moved 'em down to the barn. She always does that when the pups get older."

Wesley stared at her cousin's bundled form. She

could feel the color rising in her face. "Why didn't she tell me she was going to move them?"

" 'Cause it ain't no big deal, Wes. Just go down and see for yourself if you're so worried."

Wesley rushed down the stairs and into the mud room. She stuffed her feet into her boots, threw on her coat, then burst from the house. She ran down to the barn, her coat undone and flapping behind her. She struggled with the sliding door on the barn, kicking it impatiently several times to loosen the ice that had formed on the runners in the night.

Inside, the barn was dark and sweet with the smell of cedar shavings. Wesley strained her eyes, seeing nothing at first, save the orange cones of light from the heat lamps in the kennels. She slid the door shut then felt around for the switch, turning the overhead lights on with a snap.

The dogs whined expectantly. They stood at the front of their kennels, their names engraved on small wooden plaques and fastened with silver wire to the doors: Riley, Cisco, Zest, Beamer, Sky and Holly. Four girls and two boys.

"Piper," Wesley called out.

A sharp "yip" sounded from the far end of the barn.

Wesley walked along the concrete aisle, the dogs watching her with curious interest. She had grown to know each of them well, their distinct personalities revealing themselves over time. Riley was the patriarch.

Holly was serious and maternal. Cisco was the clown. Beamer was quiet and inscrutable. Zest liked to bark. And Sky was gentle and loving. She liked Sky the best. She nicknamed her "Skupper."

Wesley heard another sharp "yip" from the far end of the barn, followed by a chorus of plaintive puppy whines. When she reached the kennel marked HOLLY, Wesley peered inside. Holly was there, and so were the other pups, but she couldn't see Piper. "Piper," she called out, her voice trembling with the beginnings of panic. There was a muffled whine and the scrabbling of small paws on wood.

And then Wesley saw her — or at least the back end of her — the puppy's red bob of a tail sticking out between the wooden plank of the whelping pen and the stone wall of the barn.

"Oh no!" Wesley cried, throwing the kennel door open and rushing over to where the puppy was wedged. She pulled the wooden plank as hard as she could with her hands, dislodging the frightened pup, who scrambled up and over the plank, shaking herself clean of shavings. "You poor, poor thing!" Wesley soothed.

But Piper seemed no worse for her predicament, licking Wesley enthusiastically on the face.

"You found the puppies, I see," Aunt Cindy said through the kennel door.

"She was stuck. Poor thing," Wesley clucked.

"We have to get Uncle Norman to fix that pen. It's dangerous."

Aunt Cindy nodded. "I'll get him to fix it while we're at the vet. They're getting their needles today."

"I can come, right?" Wesley asked, slipping the puppy into the pocket of her kangaroo jacket. She zipped her coat halfway so that only Piper's head could be seen.

"You're going to turn that pup into a lap dog," Aunt Cindy admonished.

Wesley looked at the puppy anxiously. Was it wrong to love her too much? I won't do it when she gets bigger, she promised herself. "Come on, Pipes," she said. "Let's go get that lazy Cassel out of bed."

Upstairs, Cassel still lay in a bundle on her bed. Wesley sneaked into the room, placing Piper on top of Cassel's comforter. "Go get her," she whispered.

Piper scrambled over the bundle, grabbing the edge of Cassel's blanket and tugging with all her might. Then she licked and nipped at Cassel's face.

"Ahhhh! Get outta here, you crazy mutt!" Cassel yelled, laughing and covering her face with her blanket.

Piper continued to pull and tug on the blanket, her bright blue eyes twinkling with mischief. Wesley joined in with a pillow, pounding ruthlessly at the howling bundle until Cassel jumped out of bed.

"Okay, okay! I'm up, you crazy freaks!" Cassel grabbed her pillow and started hitting at her cousin,

her blonde hair frizzing wildly around her face.

Piper barked excitedly, then launched off the bed, catching Cassel's pillow with her teeth in midflight. The pillow ripped with a loud tearing sound, the feathers bursting out in a big white cloud that filled the room. The girls looked at each other in shock, then dropped to the floor, screaming with laughter. Piper barked furiously, the feathers falling all around them like giant flakes of snow.

"We're in for it now!" Cassel shrieked and laughed.

"What on earth!" Rosemary gasped, appearing at the bedroom door.

The girls sat up in fright, the feathers still drifting languidly in the air. Wesley grabbed Piper, who continued to pull and tug at the gutted pillow. "It was an accident, Mom," she quickly explained. "We were just trying to get Cassel out of bed." She yanked on the pillow case, trying to tear it from the puppy's teeth.

Rosemary stood with her hand over her mouth, trying to cover a smile. She frowned deliberately, but could not hide the amusement in her voice. "Well, you'd better get the vacuum and clean this up before Aunt Cindy comes in from the barn." She frowned again, then turned from the room and started to laugh.

The girls managed to get most of the feathers cleaned up before Aunt Cindy called them downstairs. The puppies were already in a crate in the car, ready to go to the vet. Wesley added Piper to the litter, then buckled herself in the back seat next to the crate.

"What's in your hair?" Aunt Cindy asked, peering suspiciously at Wesley from the rearview mirror of the car.

Wesley smoothed her hair with her hands, pulling out several feathers and attempting to stuff them in her pocket. "Must have been from feeding the biddies this morning," she lied.

"Were you standing on your head in the coop?" Aunt Cindy asked sarcastically.

"Must have been," Cassel quipped, then snorted through her hand.

"What's going on?" her mother demanded.

"Oh, nothing," Cassel said, giving her cousin a wink.

The ride to the vet's was filled with giggles and concealed messages. Aunt Cindy gave up trying to decipher the girl's conversation. She turned on the radio instead, the strains of country music crackling from the dashboard of the old blue Chrysler.

When they reached Dr. Voight's office, Aunt Cindy pulled up next to a pickup truck. She revved the engine for good measure, then turned off the car, the engine sputtering and coughing before falling silent. Wesley carried Piper inside, squeezing her into the pocket of her kangaroo jacket like before. Cassel wanted to do the same with one of the other pups, but Aunt Cindy refused, insisting on keeping the rest of the litter in the crate.

"It ain't fair!" Cassel stormed, bursting into the clinic, Wesley walking aloofly behind her.

"Well, Cassel," Wesley began. "Maybe if you took a little more responsibility with the pups you would have the chance to —" She stopped short. There was someone already sitting in the clinic waiting room, staring at the girls as they came in. It was Kyle Anderson!

## 7.

## TROUBLE

 "Hi Wesley," Kyle said, a big, gap-toothed grin on his face. He wore jeans and a blue sweater with a matching baseball cap, his sandy-colored hair sticking out like straw at the sides. There was a cardboard box at his feet.

"K-Kyle," Wesley stammered in surprise, completely forgetting the invaluable advice she was going to bestow upon her younger cousin.

"Is that your pup?" Kyle asked, pointing to Piper, who struggled to get free from Wesley's jacket.

"Yeah," Wesley said with a nervous laugh.

"She's cute. Red merle, right?"

"Yeah." Wesley could feel the color rising in her cheeks.

Cassel looked at her cousin suspiciously. "She's a runt."

Kyle shrugged. He looked right at Wesley. "Nice blue eyes, though."

Wesley's face started to burn, the hair on the back of her neck tingling. "Those your pups?" she managed to say, pointing to the box at Kyle's feet.

"Yeah. Wanna see 'em?" He reached over, pulling the flaps open. There were six little black and white pups staring mournfully from inside the box.

"Oh! They're adorable!" Wesley exclaimed, forgetting her shyness.

"Border Collies. They'll be seven weeks in a couple of days."

"We've got seven pups — all different colors," Cassel boasted. "They're seven weeks old today."

"Have they had their needles yet?" Wesley asked, pointing to the puppies in the box.

"Just got 'em," Kyle said. "I'm waiting for my dad to finish talking with the vet."

Aunt Cindy banged and pushed the clinic door open with her foot, hauling the crate in with one hand. "Thanks for helping with the door, girls," she admonished.

Wesley rushed over to the door and held it open while her aunt struggled inside. Kyle's father appeared from one of the offices. He nodded curtly at Aunt Cindy, then motioned for his son to come along. Aunt

Cindy nodded stiffly back.

"I guess I'll see you at school," Kyle said to Wesley. He picked up the box of puppies, made a point of saying hello to Aunt Cindy, then followed his dad out the door.

"Border Collie folk," Aunt Cindy said under her breath. "Is that John Anderson's son? He seems nice."

"Yeah," Cassel said knowingly, nudging Wesley in the ribs. "Kyle. He's *real* nice."

"Get lost, you little twerp," Wesley snapped. She could feel herself blushing again.

"We're ready for the Aussie pups," Dr. Voight called from the examining room.

The receptionist motioned for Aunt Cindy to go in. Wesley followed, Piper still nestled in the pocket of her jacket.

The pups yelped loudly when they got their vaccinations. Wesley couldn't help but feel nervous when it was Piper's turn, closing her eyes as Dr. Voight stuck the long silver needle under the puppy's skin. But Piper didn't seem to feel a thing, looking around the room as though it was just another place for her to explore.

"Not bad for a runt, huh?" Wesley said proudly.

The doctor inspected the pup, holding her up to the light to see her eyes. "She's not much of a runt anymore," she said. "She's just about caught up with her litter mates. And she's a sharp little thing, too." She handed the puppy back to Wesley, who tucked her into the pocket of her jacket. "Whatever you're doing, keep it up."

Wesley beamed with pride. She couldn't wait to get home to tell her mom about Piper's visit to the vet. She would tell her everything Dr. Voight said. She imagined how her mom would listen intently, asking questions in all the right places.

But Rosemary was busily baking in the kitchen when Wesley got home, the timer buzzing, hot trays clattering on top of the stove. While Wesley gushed about the puppy, her mom only nodded absently, her mind on cookies and cleaning and packing Christmas tins for the neighbors.

"Never mind," Wesley said flatly when Rosemary asked her the same question for the third time. "You don't care anyway." She reached to grab a handful of cookies from a cooling rack on the table.

"Not the good ones!" Rosemary reprimanded, rushing over with a small plate of castoffs.

"Thanks," Wesley grumbled. "I get the rejects."

The timer buzzed. Rosemary ignored her daughter's remark, turning her attention to the stove. "Did you do your homework, dear?" she asked mechanically, removing hot cookies from the tray.

"It's the holidays," Wesley said with irritation. "I don't have any homework."

"Christmas is coming. Only a few more days now."

"Yeah," Wesley muttered. She broke off a small

piece of shortbread and fed it to Piper. "I know you care," she whispered to the pup, then shuffled quietly upstairs.

» «

Winter stretched on in the county, the snow falling seamlessly for days on end. Christmas came and went with the usual assortment of toys and books and bath oil beads. There was a moment of temporary panic when Wesley went missing, only to be found curled up with Piper and the biddies in the chicken coop.

"It isn't right without Dad," she said.

It took Rosemary some time to convince her to come back to the house. She lured her from the coop with a pocketbook about magic that she had been saving as a New Year's surprise. Wesley spent the rest of morning on the couch with her nose buried in the book, Piper sleeping comfortably in her lap.

And there was the terrifying week when Mr. Sharp lost a sheep to the hunger of the coyotes. Wesley watched over the biddies with greater vigilance then. She'd seen the blood — a dark shock of red staining the clean white snow.

Most of the puppies were spoken for, the owners visiting on several weekends before taking them to their new homes. For whatever reason, Aunt Cindy sold the big pup that she had said had promise. She didn't explain why, just mumbled something about "disposition." By the time three months had passed, there were only two puppies left: Piper and the little blue merle that Cassel had named Flash.

One day, Wesley arrived home from school to find her aunt and Piper in the small corral by the barn. Aunt Cindy stood with her shepherd's crook in her right hand, her small flock of sheep moving nervously around the pen. Piper was sniffing the air excitedly, trotting along one side of the corral. The sheep moved in quick bursts in front of her, not sure of the pup's intentions.

"She's definitely interested," Aunt Cindy said, pointing her crook toward Piper.

Cassel soon joined them, and together the two girls watched with curiosity as Piper explored her effect on the sheep.

At dinner that night, the conversation was animated and lively.

"You should have seen her, Mom," Wesley raved. "She seemed to really know what to do, trotting along the fence and all."

"She did seem to take quite an interest," Aunt Cindy added. "Flash, on the other hand, hid behind my legs, shaking."

"Piper didn't shake," Wesley boasted. "She really kept her eye on the sheep — watching them everywhere they went. I just know she's going to be a champion."

Everyone burst out laughing. Wesley hung her head, a shy grin on her face. Even she couldn't help laughing at herself — just a little.

» «

After many such preliminaries, Aunt Cindy reluctantly admitted that Flash wouldn't amount to much in the way of a herding dog. He didn't seem to have the drive or the desire. She sold the pup to a sheep farmer named Mike Fletcher up on Big Island. He knew about the pup's champion bloodlines and felt it was worth the chance. Aunt Cindy wished him luck and promised to help out in any way she could.

Wesley watched the man leave, Piper standing beside her. "We've just got to work hard, Pipes, so Aunt Cindy will let you stay," she said, leaning over and scrubbing the pup behind the ears.

Piper looked up as though she understood, her blue eyes searching Wesley's face. She was growing so quickly, Wesley thought. She was still the puppy they had fought to save on that snowy night in November, but she was entering what Aunt Cindy called a "gawky stage."

Her legs seemed too long for her body. She ran at an awkward angle, leaning over to one side, tripping over her feet in the process. Her head was changing shape, which only added to her clownish looks. Her puppy fuzz was being rapidly replaced by adult fur, the longer, smoother hair pushing up through the fuzz like the quills of a porcupine, creating a strange halo of hair around her slender form. She had even lost a few teeth, Wesley nicknaming her "The Hockey Player."

"Come on, Pipes," Wesley said. "We've got chores to do."

Wesley disappeared into the mud room to grab the feed pail, Piper waiting patiently on the bottom step outside the door. Wesley reappeared with the pail and the two ran down the hill to the chicken coop, skidding and sliding in the snow. When they reached the pen, Wesley stepped over the wire fence. Piper attempted to scrabble underneath.

"Aaaahhh!" Wesley shouted in reprimand. "Come around, Pipes." She opened the gate to the chicken pen, patting her hand encouragingly against her thigh. "Come on."

Piper trotted happily through the opening. She watched intently as Wesley filled the pail with feed, then called the chickens from the coop. The chickens clucked and scratched in the snow, Piper standing happily among them as she had done on so many mornings before.

"You know the routine, Pipes," Wesley said, placing the pail on the ground. "We have to check for eggs." She bent down, then disappeared inside the coop. When she crawled back out, her pockets filled with warm eggs, Piper was gone. The chickens

scratched complacently in the snow.

Wesley checked behind the coop. Piper wasn't there. "Here Pipes!" she called. She hopped over the wire and ran down to the barn. "Pi-per!" she yelled.

Cassel appeared from the house. Wesley waved frantically from the barn. Cassel waved back, then clumped down the lane. Wesley ran to meet her halfway.

"What's going on?" Cassel asked.

"I can't find Piper," Wesley panted, her face crumpled with worry. "I've looked everywhere and she's gone."

"Oh, we'll find her," Cassel said confidently.

"But what if she ran to the woods?" Wesley choked. "A little puppy like that —"

Cassel looked at her cousin in horror, remembering the coyotes. "Piper!" she suddenly shouted. "Here Pipes!" She ran around the barn, yelling, Wesley running and calling out beside her.

"Come on!" Cassel said at last. She grabbed Wesley by the sleeve and pulled her down the lane. They stumbled through the snow, pushing through a group of small pine trees by the path that cut through Mr. Sharp's property to the woods.

"What's that?" Cassel asked, jerking Wesley to a stop and pointing across the field.

Mr. Sharp's sheep were moving in frantic waves across the field. They bawled warnings through the air, their feet pounding the ground. A small group sprang from the flock, leaping through the air. Piper appeared, barking and scrabbling excitedly, chasing the frenzied sheep across the field.

"Piper, no!" Wesley shouted, running toward the fence. She waved her hands wildly over her head.

"Piper! Get over here!" Cassel yelled.

Piper instantly turned and ran toward the girls, the sheep thundering ahead of her.

"She's chasing them right to us!" Cassel cried.

"No! Piper, no!" Wesley screamed, jumping onto the top rail of the fence. She swung her legs over the rail, her heart pounding in her ears. She was almost over the fence, her leg poised in the air, when it happened.

The sheep exploded in every direction. One of the animals crashed headfirst into the fence, snapping the thick rail in half. Wesley hurtled to the ground with a sickening thump, collapsing in a motionless heap in the snow. The sheep slumped heavily beside her, its legs crumpled beneath its woolly body, its lifeless head flopping to one side. A gunshot blasted through the air.

"Wesley!" Cassel screamed. She stumbled over the broken rail, tearing her coat as she fell to the ground beside her cousin.

Piper came running up just as Mr. Sharp appeared, a rifle in his hands. "What in the name of —?"

Wesley groaned and rubbed her head, her face twisted with pain. Her pockets oozed yellow with the yolks of crushed eggs. She turned to look at the sheep and was met by Piper's wet tongue on her face. "Piper!" she sobbed.

Mr. Sharp grabbed Piper by the scruff and shook her, the puppy yelping in surprised terror.

"Please don't hurt her, Mr. Sharp! Please!" Wesley begged. "She doesn't know any better. She's just a pup!"

"It wasn't her fault, Mr. Sharp," Cassel cried.

Mr. Sharp stared at the children, the puppy hanging stiffly from his hand, her eyes rolled back in her head.

"It's my fault," Wesley sobbed. "I didn't watch her. I left her alone outside. She didn't mean to hurt the sheep." She looked up at him, her face wild with fear.

"I could've shot her," Mr. Sharp barked. "Don't you think I have enough trouble without this dog chasing and killing my sheep?"

"Please, Mr. Sharp," Wesley pleaded. "She didn't know any better. I'm the one who should be punished."

Mr. Sharp stared hard at Wesley. Wild tendrils of wheat blonde hair had sprung loose from her braids and curled around her face, just the way his granddaughter's sometimes did. He muttered under his breath, shoving the puppy into Wesley's arms, then kneeled down to inspect the sheep. He moved its woolly head to one side, and then the other, its dark blue tongue protruding from its velvety muzzle.

"Neck's broke," he announced solemnly.

The girls watched in horrified silence. There was something unreal about the dead sheep. It looked strangely peaceful with its eyes closed—like it was sleeping.

"You all right?" Mr. Sharp asked Wesley, his eyes still focused on the sheep.

"I think so," Wesley mumbled into her jacket. She could not bear to look at Mr. Sharp. She could not bear to look at the sheep lying in a heavy heap on the ground. She buried her face in Piper's warm fur.

"You kids get outta here," Mr. Sharp suddenly growled. "And take your dog with you. I don't want to see you on my property again."

Wesley nodded obediently, her face burning with shame. Everything swirled in front of her, the white form of the sheep blurring through her tears into the snow. She picked her way blindly over the broken rail, Cassel following carefully behind her. Once over the fence, Wesley turned to face Mr. Sharp. "I'm sorry," she whispered, then walked slowly up the lane to the house.

# 8.

## CHORES

Mr. Sharp proved to be a lot calmer about the sheep than either Aunt Cindy or Rosemary.

"How am I supposed to pay for this?!" Wesley's mother screamed, then burst into tears.

It was the first time Cassel had ever heard her aunt yell. Wesley stood unmoving, staring mutely at the floor.

Aunt Cindy phoned Mr. Sharp to apologize and to pay for the damage. Mr. Sharp acted as though nothing had happened and even refused to take any money. Aunt Cindy offered one of the sheep from her small herding flock. Mr. Sharp would not take it. But Aunt Cindy was adamant: the girls would pay for the damage.

"I don't think Cassel should have to help," Wesley petitioned when Aunt Cindy outlined the chores. "It wasn't her fault. Piper's my dog. I'm the one who let her get away. Cassel had nothing to do with it."

"It's okay, Wes," Cassel surprised her cousin by saying. "I want to help. I was there, too. I called Piper over. That's why she chased the sheep to the fence."

"Fine. It's settled, then," Aunt Cindy snapped. "You both start chores tomorrow."

Neither Wesley nor Cassel complained when they were told to clean the kennels and do extra work around the house. They wanted to pay Mr. Sharp for the sheep. Every day after school, they would rush off the bus to change their clothes and clump down to the barn in their "work" boots — black rubber Wellingtons with salmon red soles.

The cousins made good on their promise: feeding the dogs; throwing hay to the small flock of sheep; cleaning kennels and stalls; trimming nails; brushing burrs out of fur; chipping ice from water that had frozen in the pails. They worked side by side, united in their goal to replace the sheep and reclaim their dignity. Piper followed them faithfully through everything, her awkward form changing and growing with each passing day.

And the girls were growing too, in subtle ways. Wesley was surprised one day to find her horse picture carefully hung in the spot that had caused so much trouble the first week she was there. And Aunt Cindy and Rosemary were surprised when Cassel came marching off the bus sporting a black eye because someone in the schoolyard had called Wesley a "Yankee."

For months the two cousins worked, earning ten dollars a week to pay for the damage they had caused. They saw Mr. Sharp from time to time as they walked to the barn and back, or shoveled snow from the driveway, and although he was polite, they knew that things would never be the same.

» «

The winter seemed longer than usual that year. The coyotes took greater chances, coming out in daylight hours and skulking at the edge of the dusky woods behind the barn. At night, their hungry cries would begin, the sound of gunshots echoing in the dark. Wesley shuddered to hear it, remembering the rifle and Mr. Sharp's anger. She would lie awake, listening, Piper barking and howling in frustration from her crate in the kitchen, until Aunt Cindy would yell for her to stop.

And then there was her mother. Sometimes, late at night, Wesley could hear her crying in her room. She felt ashamed for this, for violating the privacy of her mother's sorrow. She wanted to fly into her room and throw her arms around her. She wanted to tell her that everything would be all right, that she wouldn't always be so lonely. But Wesley could only listen in guilty silence, and pray that her mother would find consolation in the morning light.

It seemed that spring would never arrive and that the girls would never earn enough money to pay Mr. Sharp. His own sheep had already lambed before the snow had left the ground, the steam rising from new, wet bodies as the lambs greedily nursed warm milk in the last of the winter cold.

But by the time the first songbirds were bravely warbling in the naked trees, and the delicate crocuses were peeking hopeful faces through the remaining ice and snow, Wesley and Cassel had earned enough money to replace the sheep.

They could only afford a lamb, but Mr. Sharp didn't seem to mind. It was a bright young ewe — someday she would have babies of her own.

"Easy now," Uncle Norman said soothingly as he carried the quivering lamb down the lane to Mr. Sharp's field.

Wesley and Cassel walked quietly alongside, their faces serious. The path was mucky from the spring rain. The mud sucked at their boots and splattered on their pants.

"Do you think Mr. Sharp will like the little lamb, Wes?" Cassel asked in a low voice.

"I hope so," Wesley whispered, chewing nervously on her lower lip.

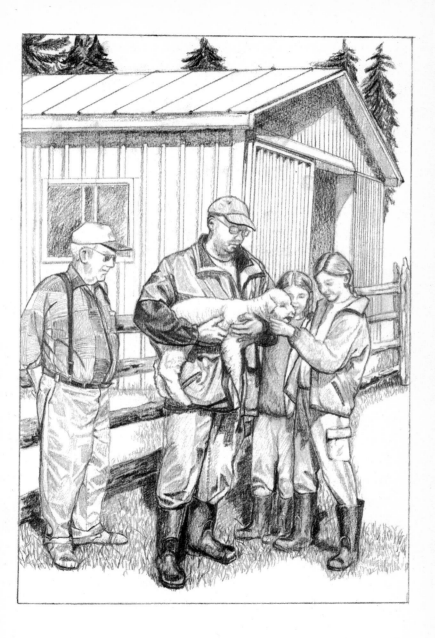

Mr. Sharp stood waiting at the end of the lane. He did not look at the girls, but took the lamb from Uncle Norman, placing it in a small pen with several of his own. The new lamb trembled, its head lowered, its gangly legs splayed awkwardly out to the sides. "Go on," Mr. Sharp said tenderly. "This is your home now." With surprising gentleness, he ran a big callused hand across the animal's back.

"Guess that's it then," Uncle Norman said.

The two men shook hands, the girls standing solemnly by. Mr. Sharp carefully fastened the latch on the gate, gave a nod to the girls, then made his way back up to the house. Wesley watched him go. He'll never forgive me, she thought.

"Come on, Wes," Cassel said. "Let's go have some fun with Piper. She's been penned up in the house all morning."

"You go on," Wesley said. "I'll be up in a minute."

Uncle Norman put his arm around Cassel. They walked up the path to the house, chattering happily about the lamb. Wesley waited until they were in the house before sneaking around the pen, past the manure pile, and through the paddock to the back of Mr. Sharp's barn. She pushed the heavy sliding door — carefully, and just slightly open — then slipped inside.

The air inside the barn was moist and close. She waited until her eyes adjusted to the diffuse light, then picked her way over to the ladder that led to the hayloft. The loft was still and sweet with the smell of hay. The spring sunlight filtered in long, gold fingers through the slats of the barn walls. In one corner of the loft, a giant pyramid of hay bales reached almost to the ceiling. From a dark beam over the hay, a thick rope snaked lazily down to the ground, tied there years ago, when Mr. Sharp's children were still young.

Wesley sat on one of the hay bales, quietly enjoying the serenity of her secret place. She stayed that way for some time, then pulled a quarter from her pocket and rolled it skillfully over her knuckles before waving her hands and making it disappear. She produced the quarter from her own ear, then rolled it over her knuckles again.

"Bravo," a voice suddenly broke the silence.

Wesley jumped, dropping the quarter to the ground. She turned to see Mr. Sharp's face peering at her from the opening in the floor. "Mr. Sharp!" she gasped. "I was just sitting up here. I wasn't going to touch anything — honest."

"Where's that pup of yours?" Mr. Sharp asked, ignoring Wesley's frantic explanation.

"She's in the house, I swear. I never leave her outside alone anymore. Ever since she chased the sheep —"

"Go get her, then," he demanded, "and meet me back in the pen behind the barn." His face disappeared down the hole.

Wesley stood for a moment, unsure of what to

think. Was Piper in trouble again? She made her way down the ladder, then ran out of the barn and to the house. She found Cassel playing with Piper on the kitchen floor. "Come on, Piper," Wesley called. The dog scrabbled across the kitchen and out the door.

"What's going on?" Cassel asked.

"I don't know," Wesley yelled over her shoulder. "But it must be something serious. Mr. Sharp said to bring Piper and meet him behind the barn." The screen door slammed behind her.

Cassel came rushing out of the house, wrestling with her yellow spring jacket. She raced to catch up with her cousin and Piper, who was dancing excitedly around Wesley's feet.

Mr. Sharp stood in the pen at the back of the barn. He had a cap pulled low to his eyes. In his hand he held a long wooden crook. There was a small group of sheep huddled in one corner of the pen.

"What's going on?" Wesley asked.

"School!" Mr. Sharp said.

# 9.

# SCHOOL

"School?" the girls exclaimed in unison.

"Yes, school!" Mr. Sharp repeated. "If you're going to keep that pup, she'd better learn a thing or two." He unlatched the gate to the pen and whistled for Piper. "Come on pup, let's see what you're made of."

Piper hesitated at the gate. She looked back at Wesley in confusion.

"It's okay, Pipes," Wesley reassured her. "Go on."

Piper walked cautiously into the pen, sniffing the air suspiciously. The sheep huddled together, eyeing the dog.

"Go on, Piper," Mr. Sharp said. "Have a look-see."

Wesley and Cassel exchanged bewildered looks,

then shrugged, climbing to the top rail of the pen to watch. Piper zigzagged nervously to the left of the small group of sheep. She trotted instinctively along the length of the corral until she was behind the flock. One of the sheep suddenly whirled around, stamping its foot in the mud. Piper spun away and around the group, approaching them from the other side. Then she suddenly darted at one of the sheep, nipping it below the hock. The sheep turned on the puppy, butting her angrily with its head.

Mr. Sharp chuckled as Wesley gasped. Piper rolled over in the mud, her gangly legs sprawling. The pup sprang quickly to her feet, rushing the sheep again. Again the sheep charged, only this time Piper managed to dodge out of the way. The sheep spun around, stamping its foot in warning. It lowered its woolly head in challenge.

Piper stood fast as the sheep charged. It butted the young pup, tumbling her violently to the ground. Piper shook her head and scrambled to her feet. But before she could right herself, the sheep charged again, knocking her to the ground with a sharp yelp.

"It's gonna kill her!" Wesley burst out in horror.

Mr. Sharp lunged toward the sheep, using his crook to push it out of the way. He quickly grabbed Piper and tucked her skillfully beneath one arm. He carried her over to where the girls sat on the fence. "She's got something, all right," he said, laughing. "I knew it the day she chased them sheep in the field." He handed Piper to Wesley.

Wesley fawned over the pup, running her hand over Piper's head and fretting terribly when she found blood.

"She'll be all right," Mr. Sharp assured her. "She'll get a lot worse than that in her career. Bring her back tomorrow — same time."

Wesley stared at Mr. Sharp in confusion. "I didn't know you knew about this stuff," she said awkwardly.

Mr. Sharp scrubbed at his chin, chuckling. "I know some."

Wesley eyed him with curiosity, then hopped down from the fence. "Same time tomorrow," she said. She put Piper on the ground, then turned and ran to the house, Piper and Cassel running wildly beside her.

When they reached the mud room, Wesley grabbed Aunt Cindy's red metal tack box. She unlatched the fasteners and opened the lid, digging around for the purple antiseptic powder she'd seen her aunt use on the sheep when they got cut.

"What do you think made Mr. Sharp want to train Piper?" Cassel asked, trying to hold the dog still between her knees.

Piper panted and whined with excitement, her eyes trained on the mud room door.

"I don't know," Wesley mused, dusting the purple powder on Piper's cut. "But I'm not complaining.

He seems to know what he's doing."

"I guess he ain't mad about the sheep no more."

"I guess not," Wesley said, tossing the powder bottle back into the tack box. "Look at her," she said, pointing at the dog. "She doesn't even care about the fact that she got cut. She just wants to get back out there and start herding those sheep again."

Piper whined softly, her pink tongue lolling out the side of her mouth. Her eyes shone with a strange new intensity.

"This is how it starts," Cassel said, knowingly.

» «

That night at dinner, the girls could hardly contain their enthusiasm. They recounted every detail of Piper's first lesson: how she stood her ground, how the sheep responded, and what Mr. Sharp had said. Surprisingly, it was Aunt Cindy who seemed the most thrilled. "If Mr. Sharp said she's got talent, I'm not going to argue. Tell me exactly what he said again."

Wesley explained everything again, searching for more and different details that she may have forgotten the first time.

"How come Mr. Sharp never told us he could train dogs?" Cassel asked her mother.

Aunt Cindy shrugged. "He hasn't done it for years and years. Long before either of you were born."

"But how come he never told us?" Cassel persisted. "And why doesn't he have dogs of his own?"

"Oh, you know," Aunt Cindy sighed. "Things happen. His wife died and all his kids grew up. And then he lost those two dogs of his — one after the other."

"Yeah. That was a strange thing," Uncle Norman said.

"What were their names again …?"

"Chili and Striker," Uncle Norman offered.

"No, not Chili … That was Hal Smith's dog. It was something else."

"Bummer," Uncle Norman said.

"Bummer!?" Cassel snickered at the name.

"That's it," Aunt Cindy confirmed. "Striker and Bummer."

"What happened to them?" Wesley asked.

"Well …," Aunt Cindy pushed her dinner plate to the middle of the table and sipped her coffee. "One got hit by a car — that was terrible — and the other one …" Here she hesitated, searching for the right words. "Well, it went missing, I guess."

The girls exchanged serious looks.

Rosemary raised her eyebrows. "What do you mean, 'went missing'?"

"Well … the dog just never came in one night. Al looked for her everywhere — asked all over the county thinking maybe someone had seen her or picked her up. Everyone knew Bummer. She was quite a dog.

And then, a couple of weeks later, he found her in the back field. He never knew what happened — if she got in a fight, or if she died of something else and was torn to pieces later."

Rosemary clutched the buttons at the top of her blouse. "Coyotes?" she asked.

"Yeah, maybe," Aunt Cindy said. "Or coydogs. That's what some people were saying."

"What's a coydog?" Wesley asked.

"Half-breed — part coyote, part dog. Vicious things — and bold, too. They're not afraid of people the way coyotes are. I've seen a few around here myself." Aunt Cindy stared out the kitchen window for a bit, then took another sip of her coffee.

"In any case, it was too late to tell what had happened — what with the rain and all — and Al sure didn't want to talk about it. He started carrying a rifle after that."

"That was a strange thing," Uncle Norman said again, shaking his head.

Everyone sat in silence for a moment.

"How awful," Rosemary finally said.

Aunt Cindy nodded her head. "Anyway, he hasn't done a thing with the dogs ever since," she continued. "And it's a shame, because he was one of the best. Took trophies from here to Gaspé. I was thinking to send Piper over to Tom Thompson's down in Waupoos, but if Al Sharp is willing to train her, that's fine by me."

Wesley looked at her aunt in surprise. It was the first she had heard of any plans to have Piper professionally trained. Uncle Norman winked at her from across the table.

"Did Mr. Sharp say how much it'll cost?" Rosemary tentatively asked.

Wesley shook her head. "He just said come back tomorrow at the same time."

"Don't worry about it, Rose," Aunt Cindy said. "I'll have a talk with him tomorrow. I would have had to pay Tom anyway."

» «

That night, Wesley put Piper on the leash when she went down to feed the biddies. She couldn't stop thinking about Mr. Sharp and his dogs. She could hear the coyotes barking deep in the black woods. The air was heavy with spring rain, the smell of the lake mingling with the mossy green scent of new life pushing up to meet the darkening sky. Piper tugged on the leash, her tongue curling as she panted. Twice Wesley had to jerk her back and walk in a circle, just to make her mind. "You stay close to me, okay, Pipes," she said, tightening her hold on the leash.

» «

The next day, Mr. Sharp was waiting, crook in hand, the sheep mingling nervously in the pen. Wesley lifted the latch on the gate to let Piper in.

"You too," Mr. Sharp said. "Today's your first lesson." He handed Wesley the crook. It was smooth and worn in the place were he held it, and at the top, where it curved, there were two small initials engraved in the wood.

"A.S.," Wesley read out loud. "Is that you, Mr. Sharp?"

Mr. Sharp nodded. "It was my dad's, first: Avery Sharp. He gave it to me when I was about your age. Letters worked the same for me."

"Al Sharp," Wesley confirmed. She tested the weight of the crook.

Mr. Sharp moved her hand, showing her how to hold the crook properly. "How does that feel?"

Wesley held it out, stiffly at first, but soon relaxed into a more natural stance. "Feels all right."

"Good." Mr. Sharp adjusted his cap. "You have to work with the dog's natural drive," he started explaining right away. "She wants to herd the sheep — it's her instinct. The key is to get her to do it for you, not herself."

Piper suddenly rushed at the sheep, grabbing a ewe by the back leg.

"Piper, no!" Wesley screamed.

Mr. Sharp laid his hand on Wesley's shoulder. "Don't let anger get the best of you," he said. "You've got to control your voice, speak with authority — without getting angry. Dog just gets confused when you're all emotional."

Wesley nodded with embarrassment, her face beginning to blush. She tried so hard to control her temper. It just didn't always work that way....

For the rest of the afternoon, Mr. Sharp stood patiently by, helping Wesley to encourage the dog's good behavior and to discourage the bad. He showed her how to control her voice, and how to use the crook to best advantage. He taught her what was acceptable in the ring and how to predict the response of both the dog and the sheep. He showed her how to keep Piper back from the sheep without breaking her natural desire to herd. By the end of the lesson, both girl and dog were exhausted.

"I don't feel like I've learned that much," Wesley said flatly, pushing her cap to the back of her head like she'd seen Mr. Sharp do.

Mr. Sharp chuckled, resting his hand on her shoulder. "It'll come. It just takes some time. That pup has talent — loads of it, that's for sure." He squinted at Wesley who stood chewing the corner of her mouth. "And so do you," he added encouragingly.

» «

Every day after school, Wesley and Piper met Mr.

Sharp in the pen at the back of the barn. When he outright refused payment for the lessons, Rosemary started sending baked goods in a small basket covered with a blue and white gingham cloth. Mr. Sharp seemed thrilled, having long ago given up any attempt at baking, his own biscuits turning out "as hard as hockey pucks," he said.

By the time summer arrived, Wesley and Piper were ready to graduate to the big field. Slowly, and with endless patience, Mr. Sharp taught the young pup the necessary skills of the herding dog: how to run along the edge of the field and loop back on the "out-run," how to change direction toward the handler for the "come by" command, and how to drive a small flock of sheep down the field through a series of gates.

And Wesley was learning too. Mr. Sharp started her with a small metal whistle, the size and shape of a quarter. He taught her how to hold the whistle between her tongue and teeth, and how to produce a clean, sharp sound. He taught her to understand the commands — just like Piper — and to control her temper so that she could work effectively with her dog and the sheep.

Cassel watched jealously from the split-rail fence as Wesley stood in the field, the long wooden crook in one hand, her baseball cap pulled low over her eyes. She gave a series of quick, high whistles as Piper trotted evenly behind the sheep, driving them neatly into a small holding pen. Wesley carefully closed the gate behind the sheep, secured the rope, then turned, waving the crook triumphantly toward Mr. Sharp, Piper leaping and dancing beside her.

» «

From time to time throughout the summer, one of the neighboring farmers would appear, leaning against the rails of the fence, squinting critically into the sun at the young girl and her dog. Piper's herding talents were generating some interest in local circles. By the end of August, Mr. Sharp felt that Wesley and Piper were almost ready for a new challenge: The Prince Edward County All Breeds Sheep Trials.

"It may be a bit premature for this level of competition," he said enthusiastically. "But the trials aren't until November. That'll give us time to work through some weak spots."

Wesley listened intently, Piper panting at her side. Had they really come this far in only one summer? She could see the change in her dog. The puppy fuzz was gone and her tiny baby teeth had been replaced with powerful canines. Her once awkward form was now gracefully proportioned, the baby fat replaced with firm, sleek muscle. Piper seemed to understand these changes, her bright, eager face keen and serious. They had learned so much. But were they really ready for the big competition?

## 10.

## A New Challenge

September decorated the county, its rich tapestry of color draped over summer's golden splendor. Despite the girls' complaints, sandals and tangled hair were replaced with dress shoes and neat shiny braids. While the little farm eased into the colder months, Wesley and Cassel endured endless days at school, daydreaming about the big event. Wesley was constantly being reprimanded, and came very close to being sent to the office when she was caught inscribing Piper's name in her history text.

Halloween arrived with much excitement, the girls dressing Piper as a clown and pushing the bonneted Goblin in a baby carriage through the streets of Picton. The houses in the small town were completely transformed, their colonial dignity offset with big bundles of corn and gauzy curtains of spider webs. On almost every step, a jack-o'-lantern grinned, hollow eyes flickering invitingly in the dark. Children ran everywhere, their shouts and laughter filtering through the streets. The girls were determined to stay out late, but had to curtail the festivities early when the rain began to fall, Piper's ruffled crepe-paper collar running brilliant green dye into her dappled red coat.

When the winter air pinched the remaining leaves from the trees, and the last of the root crop was tumbled into the cellar, it was time at last for the big trial. Piper was now a year old. She would be competing against other pups her age, including one of her siblings, and John Anderson's dog, Twist.

Mr. Sharp gave Wesley the crook, insisting that she take it with her to the competition "for good luck." He refused to come along, though, despite Wesley's pleas, mumbling something about old age and superstition and not wanting to make her nervous. He blushed deeply when she hugged him, his eyes beaming with pride as he gave her some last minute instructions. Wesley stored the crook carefully beneath her bed.

That night, the girls were nearly sick with anticipation and worry. Cassel was sent to bed early when it was discovered that she had eaten two servings of pudding before dinner and had spoiled her appetite. Wesley joined her soon after, having exhausted herself with worry over the impending day.

The cousins lay in the dark, Wesley's fingers barely touching the crook as she dangled one arm over the side of her bed. They could hear the whir of the vacuum cleaner in the living room, and Piper whining from her crate over the sound.

"What if she don't win?" Cassel's disembodied voice whispered in the dark.

"*Doesn't* win," Wesley corrected. "What if she *doesn't* win. What do you do all day at school anyway?" she admonished her younger cousin.

"Daydream — just like you," Cassel retorted smugly. "I heard about you going to the office."

"I didn't *go* to the office," Wesley protested. "I was only threatened."

"Whatever," Cassel dismissed. "Besides, I don't need school. I'm gonna be a painter, just like my dad."

"Your dad is a middle-school teacher," Wesley said dryly.

Cassel bolted upright in her bed, her outraged face pale against the dark. "He is not!" she whispered hoarsely. "He's an artist. He just teaches school for the money!"

"Okay, okay," Wesley conceded. "But even artists need an education, Cassel. It fuels the imagination." She said this with a flourish, waving her arms in front of her.

"I've got lots of fuel," Cassel asserted indignantly.

She clicked on the small light on the night table and reached under her bed. She produced a black poster-board portfolio, tied with a frayed pink ribbon. "See," she said opening the portfolio and spreading dozens of pictures across her comforter. "I drew all of these."

Wesley propped herself up on one elbow, staring at the drawings with interest. They were meticulous illustrations of animals, some rendered in charcoal, some in thick oil pastels. "When did you do all those?" Wesley asked with genuine admiration.

"Whenever you went outside to tend the biddies," Cassel answered wistfully. "Or practiced with Piper out back." She shuffled lovingly though the drawings, arranging them in an order significant to her alone.

The house was suddenly quiet. The whir of the vacuum had stopped.

"I guess we'd better get some sleep now," Wesley said softly as Cassel folded up her work and slipped the portfolio under her bed. "Tomorrow's a big day."

Wesley nestled in, the weight of the wool blankets heavy and comfortable across her shoulders. Cassel clicked off the light then rustled around, adjusting her pillows to the right height before settling in. The room was quiet, save for the constant bubble and gurgle of Cassel's goldfish aquarium.

The calm was suddenly shattered by explosive barks from downstairs. The girls shot up in their beds. They could hear Aunt Cindy yelling at Piper.

Wesley jumped from her bed and crouched to the floor, pressing her ear against the heating vent.

"What is it?" Cassel whispered through the dark.

"I don't know," Wesley said, listening intently. "Man, Piper's going crazy down there!"

"Maybe she's just nervous about the trial," Cassel offered.

"No," Wesley said, waving her cousin to be quiet. The dog barked furiously.

"Maybe she saw something, like a cat or one of Mr. Sharp's sheep," Cassel guessed.

The door to the bedroom burst open and light flooded the room.

"What are you doing up?" Rosemary demanded, her form a silhouette in the doorway.

The light caught Wesley's astonished face as she pulled her ear from the vent. "We heard Piper barking like crazy down there, Mom," she quickly explained. "We just wanted to know what was going on."

"Well, get back to bed," Rosemary ordered in an irritated voice. "It's those coyotes again. They have the whole farm spooked. "

Wesley climbed into bed, pulling the covers up to her chin. Rosemary tucked Wesley's covers firmly into the side of the bed, then leaned over to give her daughter a kiss.

"Do you think the biddies are okay?" Wesley asked quietly.

"The biddies are just fine." Rosemary ran a cool, loving hand over Wesley's hair. She looked at her daughter, the light illuminating her worried face, her skin pale against the white of her pillow. She leaned over and kissed her again. "Now go to sleep, girls," she said in a soft voice. "We all need some rest for tomorrow."

Rosemary left the room, leaving the door slightly ajar. A narrow band of light from the hall stretched across the bedroom floor, collecting in a warm pool at the foot of Wesley's bed. The commotion downstairs was over. Cassel pulled her blanket over her shoulders and rolled to face the wall. Wesley peered into the darkness, listening as her cousin's soft breathing took on the heavy rhythm of sleep. She was alone with her nervous thoughts. She wondered if Piper was nervous too.

She thought about her dad, how he used to let her climb into bed with him whenever she was lonely or scared. He would tell her stories until she fell asleep, his voice soft and low, so as not to wake her mother who lay sleeping on her side of the bed. Her mother always seemed surprised to find her there in the morning. She would laugh and insist on making pancakes for everyone, bringing the fragrant cakes into the bedroom on a small wooden tray, the glasses of orange juice balanced carefully to one side.

But now it seemed that her mother was always preoccupied with something: money, a new job, or

Wesley's marks at school. Would she ever laugh again like she used to?

Wesley thought about the house, the one that she would buy for her mother, someday. She imagined the garden in the back with its rows of herbs, and the hollyhocks nodding gently in the breeze around the front door. She imagined the shiny wooden floors, the clean plaster walls. She saw the house room by room, and always her mother's look of joy and surprise. She imagined every detail until sleep finally found her and laid its small dark hands over her eyes.

By the time the thin November light crept up to the bedroom window, Wesley and Cassel had already eaten breakfast and dressed for the day. The girls both wore overalls and white thermal shirts. Wesley donned her Toronto Maple Leafs cap, the one her dad had given her several years ago.

While Aunt Cindy and Uncle Norman loaded the car with everything they could possibly need, like extra sweaters in case it got cold, and raincoats, and even red and white mints to eat in the car, Rosemary made cheese biscuits and coffee to take along. When everything was set, Uncle Norman backed the car slowly out of the driveway. "Everybody ready?" he asked as they pulled away.

"Ready," Wesley said, straightening her cap.

The trial was being held at a farm in Waupoos. The road curved and rolled, past vineyards and apple orchards, stark and lonely in the somber landscape. From time to time, the lake appeared in bursts through the trees, the water cold and metallic against the concrete gray of the sky.

At the competition site, cars and trucks were lined bumper to bumper along the road, and there were many more parked on the front lawn of the house. People were arriving from all over, carrying blankets, and small folding chairs, and silver Thermoses full of coffee. There was a girl in a bright red sweater squinting behind a card table selling entry tickets, and a big, green tractor pulling an empty hay wagon to transport spectators through several fallow fields to the site.

While the others wrestled with their things, Wesley leashed Piper, grabbed Mr. Sharp's crook, and walked over to the table. "Wesley Philips," she said to the squinting girl.

The girl flipped through a list of names. "Wesley and Piper?" she asked.

Wesley nodded her head. The girl drew a thick pen stroke across the page, then handed Wesley an armband with a number. "Good luck," she said, smiling.

The tractor rolled up just as the others arrived with the cooler and some chairs.

"Do you mind if Piper and I walk?" Wesley asked her mother.

Rosemary nodded and smiled. She wanted to kiss her daughter, but thought better of it and climbed onto the wagon. The tractor groaned into gear and trundled slowly along the dirt path. Cassel waved from the rear, her sneakered feet dragging and bouncing against the ground.

Piper panted heavily, despite the cool air. She pressed close against Wesley's leg as they walked. Wesley reached down to stroke her ears. "It's okay, girl," she soothed.

The two walked along the path through a narrow fence row to the show site. They could see the brightly colored banners on top of the big tent snapping gaily in the wind. As they rounded the corner, the rest of the tent slowly came into view. There were people and dogs standing and sitting everywhere. There were tall rows of bleachers, and inside the tent there were tables and elaborate pet-food displays. A voice echoed over the loudspeaker announcing the first event of the day.

"Hey, Wesley!" a familiar voice called.

Wesley looked toward the sound. Kyle Anderson waved from inside the tent.

"Hey, Kyle!" Wesley said, moving through the displays toward him.

"Is that Piper?" Kyle asked with surprise. "She's really turned out." He wore a sweatshirt with a picture of a Border Collie on the front and a blue baseball cap that said "versatility."

Piper sniffed the air, panting heavily.

"Yeah," Wesley said. "She's a little bit nervous."

"I've heard a lot about her," Kyle said. "She's pretty hot, I hear."

"She's coming," Wesley agreed modestly.

"Even my dad is interested in her," Kyle glowed, "and he doesn't even *like* Aussies." He smiled sheepishly, realizing his blunder. "Well, you know how Border Collie people are," he apologized, pulling at his shirt.

"Yeah. It's okay," Wesley said, looking around the tent.

"He's got a dog entered in the trial. You're competing against him."

"Yeah, I know. I'm sure he wouldn't want you talking to me."

"Aw, he won't mind. I mean, I can talk to anyone I want," he added confidently.

Wesley nodded. There was an awkward silence, then Piper started to whine.

"Well, I guess I'd better go," Wesley said. "She's a bit antsy."

They exchanged shy waves.

"Good luck!" Kyle called out as they left the tent.

Wesley waved again in acknowledgment, then moved toward the bleachers.

Rosemary and Aunt Cindy had positioned their chairs right at the fence. They wanted to get a good view. Uncle Norman and Cassel were balanced on the very top row of the bleachers, Cassel's bright yellow toque like a beacon. She waved happily to her cousin.

The first entry was already waiting at the side of the field near a small pen used for holding the extra sheep. Outside the pen, an old claw-foot bathtub stood at the ready, filled to the brim with water for the competing dogs. Next to the bleachers was a small, gray building that housed the announcer and the judges. Across the field, a man and his dog were driving a small flock of sheep into position.

The loudspeaker crackled, announcing the first contestant. The crowd murmured in anticipation. It was John Anderson and his little Border Collie named Twist.

Mr. Anderson moved away from the holding pen and stood by the marker at the front of the judge's booth. He held an old shepherd's crook in his left hand. Twist crouched low beside him, watching his every move. The sheep handler at the far end of the field gave a signal and the judges nodded for Mr. Anderson to begin.

With a flick of her owner's hand, Twist shot away. She made a long arc down the right side of the field, then quickly moved across the back of the field behind the sheep. A short high whistle and Twist slowed to an even trot.

The sheep began to move toward the crowd in a fluid group. Behind them, the dog wove back and forth, driving the flock down the field. As they neared the first panel, one of the sheep broke away from the group. Mr. Anderson thumped his crook on the ground, shouting loudly. Twist shot alongside the sheep, forcing the animal back into the flock. Mr. Anderson whistled again and the dog successfully guided the sheep through the first two obstacles.

"They're good," Aunt Cindy said, shaking her head. "John Anderson's the one to beat."

Rosemary watched the field, biting her nails in silence.

When they reached the third panel, three of the sheep broke out of the group and ran in the opposite direction. The crowd groaned loudly. Mr. Anderson yelled and whistled while Twist ran frantically from side to side. By the time the dog managed to regroup the sheep, they had already missed the third panel and were halfway to the small holding pen at the front of the field.

Mr. Anderson walked calmly up to the pen and opened the gate. He stretched his crook to guide the sheep as Twist drove them in. When the last sheep was through, he carefully closed the gate. The audience clapped and cheered as Mr. Anderson gave a slight bow and a tip of his hat. He reached over to pat Twist who jumped to meet his hand. They walked together along the fence to the old bathtub where Twist took a long, hard-earned drink.

Wesley squinted up at Cassel who shrugged her shoulders and waved back. Then she pointed feverishly toward the field.

The second contestant was already waiting next

to the marker. It was Piper's brother, Flash, and his handler, Mike Fletcher.

The judge gave the nod and Flash ran wide to the left. But before he reached the midpoint of the field, he cut across to the other side. The handler whistled and hollered furiously, but the dog continued to run. He hit the sheep like a bowling ball, the flock exploding in every direction. The crowed gasped and moaned. Piper pulled violently at the end of her leash, barking furiously. Mr. Fletcher yelled and screamed, then waved his arms at the judges in defeat as Flash chased several sheep down the field toward the bleachers.

"Contestant number 2 — *forfeit*," the loudspeaker boomed as the renegade dog continued to chase the sheep down the field.

Two of the sheep slammed right into the orange plastic fence, a third bursting through into the lap of the astonished crowd.

Piper lurched forward, twisting out of her collar and bolting toward the loose sheep.

"Piper, no!" Wesley yelled as the dog ran to herd the sheep back into the pen. "Get down!"

Piper dropped to the ground as though shot, her head lowered. The sheep bounded away, bouncing on all fours like a sprung coil. Wesley snapped the collar on Piper, administering a series of quick, angry corrections. "What's gotten into you?" she demanded, giving Piper a shake.

Mr. Fletcher collected his hat and crook, Flash crouching submissively by his side. The sheep handlers deployed their dogs from the sidelines to gather the scattered sheep. The crowd chattered excitedly. The loudspeaker crackled again.

"Wesley Philips and ... Pi–per."

Wesley felt her front pocket for her lucky stone. It wasn't there. She frantically searched her side and back pockets, but she couldn't find the stone. "Oh no," she moaned. She grabbed her crook, then tugged on Piper's collar. She ran over to where her mother was sitting. "I forgot my lucky stone!" she cried.

"Are you sure?" her mother asked with concern. "Did you check your pockets?"

"Yes. It's not there. Maybe it fell out in the car."

"What stone?" Aunt Cindy demanded.

"My lapis lazuli — the one my dad gave me."

The loudspeaker crackled again. "Wesley Philips and Piper."

"Well, you haven't got time to worry about your stone now," Aunt Cindy said. "You're going to forfeit if you don't get out there right away."

Wesley looked anxiously at her mother, then tugged on Piper's leash. Piper jumped to her feet, her tongue hanging out one side. They walked into the field and stood by the marker. Wesley clenched the thin whistle in her teeth. She exhaled loudly, then unclipped the leash from Piper's collar and placed her left hand on the dog's head.

The judge nodded; Wesley flicked her hand. Piper shot out to the left, running purposefully along the fence until she was little more than a dot on the crest of the field. Wesley whistled high and long. The dog cut across the back of the field behind the sheep. Another short, sharp blast on the whistle and Piper slowed to an even trot, zigzagging behind the small flock.

The sheep moved through the first panel with ease, Piper driving them cleanly down the field. At the second obstacle the sheep stopped. Wesley whistled for Piper to come by. The flock widened, then compressed. Piper circled around, driving the sheep through the panel.

The flock picked up speed, trotting smoothly through the third panel, then turned in formation toward the pen. Piper drove them closer to the gate. Wesley walked slowly up to the pen, her crook extended. She grabbed the gate by the rope, opening it wide.

The sheep balked, crowding together. Wesley clucked encouragingly, stretching her crook to one side, the way Mr. Sharp had taught her. The sheep moved closer. Piper circled around, then pulled away. The sheep turned nervously. Wesley ordered Piper to lie down, so as not to scare the sheep.

One of the sheep reared and fell away from the flock. Piper dashed around, meeting it face to face. The sheep stamped and lowered its head threateningly.

Piper stood her ground while the other sheep huddled tentatively at the mouth of the gate.

"Ease up!" Wesley called to Piper, but the dog did not move. She eyed the sheep, unflinching, her back legs quivering.

"Ease up!" Wesley called again.

The sheep stamped its hoof and charged toward the dog. Piper scrambled out of the way, spun around and grabbed the sheep by the back leg.

"Piper, down!" Wesley yelled, slamming her crook on the ground.

The other sheep exploded out of the pen, knocking Wesley on her back. The gate swung shut with a bang, the crowd moaning loudly. Wesley scrambled to her feet to see Piper grab the renegade sheep by its side, trying to force it toward the pen. The sheep thrashed and kicked, then rolled to the ground, its feet stabbing the air. It flipped to one side, scrabbling to right itself. The dog whirled around to meet it again.

"Piper, no!" Wesley screamed. Piper grabbed the animal and held on, her feet swinging and skidding through the grass as the sheep bucked and bleated, clumps of wool flying all around.

Wesley rushed at the dog, hurling her crook like a javelin. It bounced firmly against Piper's back, the dog recoiling with a high-pitched yelp. The sheep sprang away, kicking and bucking wildly.

Wesley ran to the dog, grabbing her by the scruff.

She snapped on the leash, tugging forcefully on the dog's collar. She screamed at Piper to heel, then yanked her back down the field. She reached down and picked up her crook, then walked from the ring, the loud-speaker booming "*disqualified.*"

Rosemary rushed to her daughter, arms out-stretched. Wesley stiffened and pulled away. She could not look at her mother. She could not look at her aunt. She could not look at Cassel, or Uncle Norman or the horrified crowd. And she couldn't bear to look at Kyle, who stood in stunned disbelief by the big, white tent. Her face burned with shame. She hurled Mr. Sharp's crook to the ground, then turned and ran down the path, Piper running in wild confusion beside her.

"Wool puller!" a man said in disgust.

"*That's* why we don't like Aussie's," a woman re-marked knowingly. "They're so *violent.*"

"That one certainly is," the man said.

"What do *you* know?" Rosemary demanded, find-ing her voice. She folded her chair with a snap and marched away.

When the group reached the car, Wesley and Piper were already inside. Cassel placed the crook carefully in the back seat, looking at her cousin in sympathy as she buckled herself in. "The sheep was okay," she said. "It looked worse than it really was."

Wesley stared in stony silence out the window, her tear-stained face frozen in the light.

# 11.

## BEGINNING AGAIN

"Please just give her another chance," Rosemary implored Aunt Cindy who sat unyielding at the kitchen table.

Wesley huddled next to her mother, her face red with emotion. Cassel perched on the edge of her seat, trying to read her mother's expression. Uncle Norman remained silent, staring intently at his coffee mug.

"She's a liability, Rosemary," Aunt Cindy answered without emotion. "You can't have a dog attacking the sheep like that. You saw how she went for that animal."

"But you said yourself that it could happen to any dog," Rosemary persisted. "It was a new, scary environment — all those people and the sheep practically jumping into our laps."

"What if she goes for someone else's animal some-time?" Aunt Cindy asked grimly.

"I just can't believe we should give up on her like that — after all the work Wesley has done," Rosemary petitioned. "It just doesn't seem right."

Aunt Cindy sat unflinching, staring straight ahead. "She'll make someone a good pet."

Wesley's jaw dropped in disbelief. "Good pet?" she choked. "You mean, you want to sell her?" She turned anxiously to her mother, her eyes welling with tears. "Mom, you can't let this happen! You know Piper isn't meant to be a pet. She's mine. I trained her! I'll just work harder. She won't do it again."

Rosemary looked at her sister, her face crumpled with anguish. "Can't you just give her another chance?"

Wesley turned to her aunt. She tried to stop the anger from coming. She tried to stop the rage from swelling up inside her, choking her throat and flood-ing her brain. She shoved her chair away from the table, her eyes flashing, her body shaking. "You've hated her from the beginning!" she screamed. "This is just an excuse to get rid of her. Well, I won't let you do it! I won't let you! If she goes — I go!" She knocked her chair to the ground with a loud clatter as she ran out of the kitchen.

Rosemary stood in mute horror. Cassel pushed away from the table, rushing after her cousin. Aunt Cindy sighed through pursed lips.

"What does Mr. Sharp think?" Uncle Norman spoke at last.

"He said he's seen dogs do this type of thing before," Aunt Cindy answered coolly.

"There you go!" Rosemary said encouragingly. "I'm sure he has some ideas on how to fix it!"

"Sure he has some ideas. And they all sound like a hell of a lot of grief. It's like starting all over again, Rosemary — and there's no guarantee that any of it will work."

"But it can be done?" Rosemary asked hopefully.

"Yes, in theory," Aunt Cindy said grudgingly. She scowled thoughtfully into her coffee. "And what about Wesley?" she asked. "Can you handle her disappointment and anger if this doesn't work?"

"Yes," Rosemary said with conviction. "I really think it's worth a try."

There was a long, unbearable silence. Aunt Cindy looked at Rosemary's impassioned face. "All right," she said at last. "For heaven's sake, we'll give the dog another chance." She shook her head in defeat.

"Did you hear that, girls?" she hollered from the kitchen. "We're giving her another chance!"

》 《

The next time Wesley and Piper met Mr. Sharp there was a small, makeshift pen made of orange plastic fencing behind the barn.

"We're gonna start her on something a little different," Mr. Sharp said. "Just to get her thinking straight again." He opened the barn door and flushed out a small group of indignant ducks.

"Ducks?" Wesley exclaimed incredulously. "What's she supposed to do with them?"

"Herd 'em," Mr. Sharp said with a big grin. "That pup's gotta learn some respect for the order of things before she goes back into the field."

Wesley raised her eyebrows doubtfully as she entered the pen, the crook in one hand, Piper trotting obediently beside her.

The ducks waddled and quacked, looking suspiciously from Wesley to the dog. Piper sniffed the air, not knowing what to make of the strange birds.

"Okay," Mr. Sharp said. "Let's get at it!"

For weeks Wesley and Piper worked with the ducks, moving them through the pen, separating them into smaller groups, then collecting them again. Piper was obedient but reluctant. She spent the whole time with her head lowered to avoid looking at the vulnerable ducks, to avoid her predatory desires to chase and kill them.

The lessons stopped when the weather turned too cold. Mr. Sharp was happy with Piper's progress. He said that she was learning about patience, and how to achieve a goal through wisdom and experience, in-

stead of force. He promised to continue the lessons when the weather warmed up again in the spring.

» «

The whole county battened down for another winter. The summer vacationers were only a memory, leaving the snow-covered beaches and ice-studded lake to the locals. The sand dunes were abandoned to drift and ripple, the salt grasses rustling and waving in the wind. In town, some of the businesses had fastened their shutters against the cold and the snow, waiting patiently for the warmth and the fair-weather folk to arrive once again.

Wesley and Cassel resigned themselves to their studies. Rosemary started a new job as a receptionist at a local dental office. At night, she studied Introductory Business through correspondence. She worked side by side with the girls, diligently applying herself to her homework.

By February, the dreary days of winter had taken their toll on the cousins. Nothing of any importance had happened since Christmas. The girls were bored and more than just a little cabin crazy. The three stations they received on the television seemed even less inspired than ever. And to make matters worse, Goblin leapt up and broke the rabbit ears off the back of the set, reducing the screen to a thick band of white, crackling static. The girls languished on the living room floor, their glum faces propped in their hands.

The ring of the doorbell sent the cousins crashing down the hall to the front door. Cassel sprang for the doorknob, only to be grabbed by the back of the shirt and sent skidding down the hall. The girls laughed and wrestled, their sock feet slipping on the shiny wooden floor.

"I got here first," Cassel gasped, lunging forward.

"Oh no you don't!" Wesley shouted dramatically. "We have to see who it is first. You know the rules, pipsqueak."

The bell rang again, this time twice and with greater urgency. Wesley slid into the door, drawing the curtain to one side. Cassel struggled to overthrow her cousin who held her at arms length. "It's the mailman!" Wesley said with surprise. She opened the door with a *whoosh!* The two girls practically tumbled into the man.

"Parcel delivery for Wesley Philips."

"Me?" Wesley cried, her blonde hair a frizzy halo around her face. She ran her hands quickly through her hair, pushing it behind her ears.

"What is it?" Cassel asked excitedly.

"I don't know." Wesley took the small parcel from the man who shook his head and smiled before thudding down the stairs.

The parcel was wrapped in brown paper, tied neatly with a length of crisscrossed white string. Wesley stood looking at the package in stunned silence. She read her name, printed in neat blue ink. "There's no return address."

"Open it, for heaven's sake!" Cassel urged.

"It doesn't feel like much," Wesley said, judging the weight of the box in her hand. She tried to pull the string off one side, but it was too tight.

"We've got scissors in the kitchen," Cassel said, yanking on her cousin's shirt. "Come on."

The girls bustled into the kitchen. Rosemary sat reading at the table, Goblin humming contentedly in her lap. "Who was at the door?" she asked without looking up from her book.

"Wesley got a package," Cassel said.

Rosemary looked up, placing her book on the table. Wesley rummaged through the kitchen drawer: string, tape, nail file, some screws, several loose Band-Aids, a dried-out marker. "Come on," she said with frustration.

"Here they are!" Cassel shouted, holding the scissors in the air. "They were in the cutlery drawer."

Wesley took the scissors and clipped the string, discarding it on the counter. The box was heavily taped. She ran the scissors under one side, popping the brown paper open. She peeled the paper from the parcel, breaking another layer of tape. There was a small white cardboard box inside.

"Open it!" Cassel said excitedly.

By this time, Rosemary and Goblin were staring at the box with interest. Wesley popped open the top. There was pink tissue paper stuffed inside. She opened the tissue delicately. "It's a rose!" she said with surprise.

"Let me see!" Cassel whined, pulling at her cousin's arm.

Rosemary jumped up from the table, dumping the cat to the floor. She rushed over to look in the box.

"There's a little card inside," Wesley said nervously, pulling the small card from the box.

"Read it!" Cassel demanded. "Read it out loud!"

"To Wesley: Be My Valentine." Wesley's face burned scarlet. She turned away from her cousin, stuffing the card back in the box.

"It's from a boy!" Cassel shrieked.

"Well, what on earth?" Rosemary clasped her collar. "You have a beau!"

"I do not!" Wesley exploded. "I don't even know who this is from."

"Oh, don't be angry, darling," Rosemary soothed. "Let's have a look at it."

Wesley shoved the box toward her mother, her face scowling angrily. Rosemary pulled the card and the rose from the box. "Why, it's a corsage."

"It's a corsage!" Cassel squealed, jumping up and down.

Rosemary held the corsage up to the light. It was a small red rose encircled in baby's breath. It was wrapped in green florist's tape at the stem and attached to a ruffled white elastic wrist band. Rosemary looked at the card. She flipped it over, reading the lettering on the back. "Meet me at the dance on Friday. Wear this rose. Your Secret Admirer."

"Throw it away!" Wesley snapped, folding her arms indignantly across her chest.

Rosemary packed the corsage and card back in the box. She opened the refrigerator, placing the box delicately on the bottom shelf. "It'll keep better in here."

Cassel danced around the kitchen, a devilish grin on her face. "Wesley has a beau-oh, Wesley has a beau-oh!"

Wesley swung at her cousin, Cassel dodging easily out of the way. "I'm not going to wear it," she insisted. "I'm not even *going* to the dance."

Cassel made a kissing sound with her lips.

"You little psycho!" Wesley shouted, storming out of the kitchen and up the stairs.

Cassel lit after her, but Rosemary intervened before she reached the hall. "Leave her alone."

Cassel opened her mouth to protest, but Rosemary turned her around, marching her over to the table. Cassel sat down reluctantly while Rosemary pulled a tin of gingersnaps from the cupboard. She poured two glasses of milk, setting one in front of Cassel. She sat across from her young niece, dunking a gingersnap into her milk. "Now," she said, leaning forward and taking a bite of the cookie. "Who do you think it is?"

» «

By the time Wesley clunked down the stairs for dinner, the whole house knew about the rose. "Doesn't anyone have any privacy around here?" she grumbled pulling up to the table.

Uncle Norman and Aunt Cindy exchanged knowing glances across the room. Piper grinned from her crate in the corner of the kitchen, her plastic hamburger squeak toy stuffed in her mouth. Even Goblin seemed to be winking from his perch on top of the jelly cupboard.

» «

The next morning, Wesley took longer in the bathroom than usual. When she emerged, just as the bus was groaning to a stop at the end of the lane, she was dressed in her good brown velvet top and a newly washed pair of jeans, her hair tied in a neat braid down her back. She raced down the lane, her coat flapping behind her. Cassel stood in the door of the bus, lunch pail in one hand, her woolen hat pushed to one side of her head.

Wesley spent the rest of the day in school shyly considering the boys in her grade seven class. There was Steven Briggs: he'd stolen things from her desk. There was Ian McEwan: he'd pulled her braids a couple of times in history class. There was Gary Kelso and Brian Ledder, but they hung around the grade eights. There was Robbie Boyd, but he was so shy he never spoke to any of the girls. There just wasn't anyone in her class that she could imagine as her "secret admirer."

By Friday, when no one had revealed himself to her, Wesley was burning with curiosity. She skipped dinner and spent the whole time readying herself in the bathroom.

"I thought you weren't going to go to the dance?" Cassel chided, banging on the bathroom door.

The door swung open and Wesley appeared, her face inscrutable. "I changed my mind. Everyone else is going. I may as well. There's nothing else to do." She pushed past her cousin, stepping gingerly down the stairs in her black velvet dress shoes. She wore jeans and a green chenille sweater. Her hair was pulled into a high, tight ponytail at the top of her head.

"Are you wearing eye shadow?" Cassel asked, thumping down the stairs behind her.

"Maybe," Wesley said coolly. She stepped into the mud room, pulling her dress coat from the peg.

Norman waited out in the car, the engine running.

"Have a good time," Rosemary chimed, leaning over to kiss her daughter. "You look beautiful," she whispered, slipping the small box into Wesley's hand.

Wesley grabbed the box, tucked it under her coat, and bustled out the door.

"Why can't I go too?" Cassel whined from the mud room stairs.

"Because you have to stay home with Piper, Goblin and me," Rosemary said, kissing her niece on the head.

» «

The sharp lines of the gymnasium were transformed with long arcs of red and white streamers. There were red paper hearts in various sizes, taped to the walls, and an arch of bright pink balloons at the entrance. The lights were turned down low. A mirror ball revolved from the ceiling, sending thousands of reflected stars whirling around the room. Music blared from two large speakers on the stage. All around the gym, boys and girls were pressed in nervous groups against the walls.

Wesley walked into the gym, looking quickly around. She wore the rose on her left wrist, covering it shyly with her other hand. She noticed some of her classmates in a skittish group in one corner of the gym. She drifted over to where they were standing, trying to hear their conversation.

"I don't want anything to do with him," one of

the girls said. "Ryan Davis has been staring at us all night. He's such a creep." The other girls squealed in shared horror.

The song ended and another began. It was a slow song.

"Oh my God!" a girl named Doris shrieked, latching onto one of her friends. "Look who's coming this way!"

The girls giggled and laughed hysterically. Wesley turned her back to the gym.

"How's it going?" she heard Doris say with a lilt.

"Hey Doris," a boy's voice said.

The giggles crescendoed. Wesley studied one of the hearts on the wall. It had an arrow running through the middle and gold handwritten letters that said "Be Mine." She felt a hand on her shoulder.

"Do you want to dance?"

Wesley spun around to see Kyle Anderson smiling back at her.

"Kyle!" she said with surprise.

"Do you want to dance?" he asked again softly, touching the rose on her wrist.

Wesley nodded and the two floated onto the dance floor. She could feel her face burning as Kyle put one hand in hers and the other on her slim waist. She rested her hand lightly on his shoulder, her eyes trained on the gymnasium's shiny wooden floor.

"I see you're wearing the flower I sent you," he

said, trying to look into her eyes.

Wesley nodded silently, face lowered. The music slowly unfolded against them, the stars whirling around. They moved stiffly, from one foot to the other, in small, conservative circles. Kyle pulled Wesley closer, his hand pressing into the small of her back. She felt dizzy and light, her head spinning with the stars on the floor.

The music faded and diminished. Wesley turned to leave, but Kyle grabbed her hand.

"Stay for the next one," he said.

They stood on the dance floor, Kyle holding her hand, until the music started again. This time Wesley looked up from the floor. Kyle smiled back at her, the gap between his teeth showing. Wesley smiled shyly, then turned to see the other girls staring back in jealous wonder.

By the end of the night, Wesley had danced every slow song with Kyle. When the dance was over, they walked outside together, making nervous conversation. Students bustled out of the school, chattering excitedly in the chill February air. Uncle Norman was already waiting in the car, the heat turned on high.

Kyle suddenly pulled Wesley behind a clump of juniper bushes at the side of the school. "I had a great time," he said.

"Yeah, me too," Wesley mumbled, her back pressing against the brick wall of the school.

"I've been wanting to do something all night," Kyle whispered. He leaned over and quickly kissed her, missing her lips and catching the corner of her mouth.

Wesley laughed self-consciously. Kyle leaned over again, this time finding her mouth and lingering there. His lips were warm and soft. Wesley kissed him back, her mouth tingling with electricity, her head swimming.

"I want you to go out with me," Kyle said quickly.

Wesley looked at him blankly for a moment, then she understood. He wanted her to be his girlfriend. She nodded, smiling shyly. "Yes," she said.

When she reached the car, Wesley apologized for making Uncle Norman wait, secretly hoping that he had not seen her and Kyle at the side of the school.

"How was the dance?" he asked cheerfully.

"It was all right," Wesley answered demurely. She pulled the collar of her coat up around her neck and gazed out the dark window on her side of the car. They drove the rest of the way home in silence, the delicate rose, with its white ruffled band, still decorating Wesley's wrist, the feeling of Kyle's warm mouth still tingling on her lips.

When they got home, the house was dark, save for the small light over the stove in the kitchen. Piper rustled inside her crate. Wesley sneaked past her and up the stairs.

In the bedroom, Cassel was asleep, her face upturned and innocent, her mouth slightly open against the pillow. Wesley slid the rose from her wrist, pressing it firmly beneath her copy of *Little Women*. She undressed in the dark, pulling her nightgown over her head before removing her shoes and jeans. She crept into bed, pressing her warm face against the cool fabric of her pillow. She closed her eyes, the mirrored stars whirling endlessly into her dreams.

## 12.

## TRIALS

 Spring arrived in the county with a flourish. The trees burst forth overnight, their waxen buds unfurling in verdant splendor. Lambs were born, wet and steaming, tails waggling eagerly as they nursed. Everywhere, the earth sang praises in new life, its hungry fingers pushing ceaselessly up, through shimmering sand and dark soil.

Wesley stood in the middle of a large green space, shepherd's crook in one hand, baseball cap pulled low over her eyes. She whistled, high and far. Piper was a tiny speck in the distance, driving a group of sheep down the field. The sheep moved back and forth in waves as though buffeted by the wind. The sun came out in bursts behind the clouds, fusing everything with a dazzling glare.

The sheep trotted toward the pen. Wesley calmly opened the gate, swinging the jaw wide. Piper ran in half circles, arcing back and forth like a pendulum behind the sheep.

"Ease up," Wesley called to the dog, who instantly slowed to a trot, keeping her distance.

The sheep balked at the gate, woolly heads raised in suspicion. Wesley whistled sharp and quick. The dog inched toward the sheep, crawling along the ground on her belly. The sheep rolled their eyes nervously. One turned to face the dog, its head hung threateningly. Piper rose to her feet to meet the animal's challenge, her tongue hanging out like a pink flag.

The sheep dashed to the left. Piper mirrored the movement instantly, cutting the animal off from the front. The sheep spun and sprang back to the group, triggering the rest of the flock to push and leap into the pen. Wesley closed the gate, wrapping the cord loosely around the side post. She turned to face Mr. Sharp who waved approvingly from atop the fence. Piper looked expectantly toward her young handler, eyes winking.

"You're ready," Mr. Sharp announced as Wesley and the dog skidded breathlessly up to the fence.

» «

The banners draped languidly in the warm breeze at the Quinte Special Herding Trials. Smoke billowed from a barbecue, cheerfully operated by a rotund, red-faced man to the right of the entrance. Cassel and Uncle Norman stood in line, waiting to buy a hot dog.

There were locals, exchanging friendly greetings, and vacationers in bright matching outfits, looking on with keen interest. Most carried bags with pet food samples and flyers announcing the year's herding roster. There were dogs panting heavily in the shadow of a tall, gray barn, and a big, white tent with the usual array of displays and wares for sale. Aunt Cindy and Rosemary drifted in the shade of the tent, leisurely perusing the tables.

Wesley sat on the lowest step of the bleachers, Piper between her knees. She checked for her lucky stone, rolled it between her fingers several times, then patted her pocket superstitiously. She looked out over the field to where the handlers were driving the sheep into position at the end of the field. The announcer sat with the judges at a table beneath a large yellow-and-white striped umbrella at the entrance to the field. There was a trough full of water to the left.

"Ladies and gentleman," a calm voice came over the speakers. "Our first entrants in the intermediate class: Mike Fletcher and Flash."

Cassel came racing over to the bleachers, a hot dog in her hands. She sat down next to Wesley, ketchup dripping onto her pants.

Mr. Fletcher and his dog moved to the marker. The

judge nodded. Flash tore to the right, raced along the fence and disappeared behind a small rise. Mr. Fletcher whistled. The sheep began to trot, the dog appearing behind them. Flash drove the sheep down a small hill and up the other side. They moved through the first panel, twisting to the right and down another hill. The dog trotted easily behind them.

At the second obstacle, the sheep slipped suddenly to the left of the post, galloping around the opening. Mr. Fletcher shouted furiously, the dog scrambling to regroup the flock. It drove them faster, running in tight half-circles around the sheep to maintain the group. The sheep burst through the third panel and galloped toward the pen.

Mr. Fletcher opened the gate, stretching his crook to one side. The sheep rolled up to the pen, Flash zigzagging feverishly behind them. Another whistle and the dog stopped. The sheep slowed to a walk, moving purposefully toward the opening. Flash walked slowly behind them urging the sheep into the pen. One sheep walked easily through the gate, the rest balking in a skittish bundle behind. Flash moved slowly around, eyeing the animals.

Mr. Fletcher tapped one of the sheep on the back with his crook and the group leaped easily into the pen. The crowd clapped approvingly as he fastened the gate shut.

"That was a lot better than last year," Cassel mumbled through her hot dog.

Wesley nodded quietly, her eyes focused on the field.

The next entrant walked to the marker. She was a middle-aged woman with a young red Aussie named Teddy. The judge nodded and Teddy raced to the left. He tore along the fence, his ears flapping up and down. The crowd waited expectantly as the sheep huddled in a tight group on the crest of the field.

The crowd murmured, waiting for the dog to re-appear. The handler whistled high and far.

"We seem to have lost the second entrant," the announcer joked as the dog suddenly appeared running at the top of a hill in the next field.

The crowd roared. The handler threw down her crook and cupped her hands around her mouth. She hollered for Teddy to come back, but the dog kept running, disappearing again behind another small hill. The crowd chattered excitedly as the handler walked off the field, shaking her head in disgust.

"I'm up next," Wesley said nervously as the loud-speaker announced her name. She scrubbed Piper behind the ear, then grabbed her crook. She walked out to the marker, Piper trotting expectantly beside her.

The sheep waited in a bewildered huddle at the end of the field. Piper squinted against the sun, her pink tongue curling upward as she panted expectantly. The judge nodded. Wesley waited a beat, then flicked her hand, sending Piper in a long, smooth arc to the left of the field.

Piper disappeared from sight for a moment. Wesley whistled long and high. Piper appeared in the distance, trotting quickly. The sheep lurched forward at once, then tumbled down the field. The flock dipped below a hill, then reappeared, towing the dog behind. The sheep moved smoothly through the first obstacle, turning in unison toward the second.

Piper zigzagged in sharp cuts, driving the sheep through the panel. One of the sheep suddenly turned as though to double back. Wesley pounded her crook on the ground, giving a sharp, quick whistle. Piper punched toward the sheep, pulling away as the animal leapt through the panel.

The flock widened, breaking formation. Piper circled quickly around, tightening the group. She rushed to the back of the flock, clipping one of the sheep on the hock. The animal stabbed at the air with its hooves, springing forward. Two of the sheep tried to break around the panel but Piper bettered them, driving the flock in a uniform group between the posts.

Wesley walked up to the pen and opened the gate. She stretched her crook to the side. One of the sheep turned to face Piper as she trotted toward the pen, staring at the dog menacingly.

"Piper, down!" Wesley called.

The dog dropped to her belly, eyes trained on the

sheep. The sheep stamped again. Piper rose to her feet.

"Piper, down!" Wesley shouted again.

Piper dropped to the ground, eyes unflinching. The other sheep trembled at the mouth of the pen. Piper inched toward the sheep, her head lowered. The sheep spun and bolted toward the gate, pushing the flock into the pen. Wesley slammed the gate shut, fastening the rope to the post. She turned and waved her crook triumphantly toward her family, who stood in a group on the bleachers, clapping and cheering loudly.

"A perfect run," the loudspeaker announced.

Piper raced across the field and took a flying leap into the middle of the water trough, the crowd hooting and hollering with approval. She paddled around happily, lapping at the cool, clean water.

Seven more entrants took to the field, each with their merits and their mistakes. By the end of the day, the scores were tallied on the big slate board behind the bleachers. Wesley and Piper were at the head of the group. They had taken the lead.

But the competition was not over yet. They would have to beat many more dogs the next day in order to win the trophy.

» «

When Wesley got home that night, she found a gift on her bed. It was wrapped in smooth, cream-colored tissue, tied with a matching ribbon. There was a small card with her mother's handwriting. "To Wesley."

Cassel sat across from her, watching with intense interest.

The ribbon pulled away smoothly in Wesley's hands. She unfolded the tissue, revealing a red felt bomber jacket. It was heavy and soft, with a shiny brown satin liner. There was a small image of a plane on the front over the breast pocket with the word "Spitfire" embroidered in neat blue letters.

Wesley ran her finger over the letters, her eyes filling with tears. She looked up to see her mother standing in the doorway of the bedroom, a small, expectant smile on her face. Wesley rushed across the room. "Oh Mom, it's beautiful," she whispered, her arms held fast around her mother's neck.

» «

The next morning, Wesley insisted on arriving early to the show site. Cassel grumbled and complained, but dressed and came along just the same.

Piper was registered in a higher class, competing against more experienced dogs. She took to the field with a vengeance, her run nearly perfect, save for a terrible moment when it seemed that she would rush one of the sheep. Wesley raised her crook threateningly, and Piper backed down. They finished without a fault, easily securing first prize.

"We need to celebrate with ice cream!" Rosemary said excitedly, stuffing the cooler into the trunk.

Wesley leaned calmly against the car, holding her new red jacket. Aunt Cindy chattered away beside her. It was the first time Wesley had ever seen her so excited. Cassel stood by her mother, the first-place ribbon pinned to her shirt. She beamed in silent admiration at her cousin.

» «

The next few months were filled with trials and clinics and travel. There didn't seem to be any time to see Kyle or to go the dunes, or do any of the things they normally did in the summer. Wesley and Piper were becoming quite famous in herding circles, and were even featured in the local paper when they placed first in a trial held by the Trillium Australian Shepherd Club.

When it seemed that no other Aussie could better Piper, Mr. Sharp suggested entering an event dominated by the Border Collie set: The Nepean National Championship.

"It's not going to be easy," he warned. "This is the big competition. The one everybody waits for. And you know how those Border Collie folk can be. You had a taste of it your first time out. They don't like Aussies, or any other breed, for the most part. They don't like the way we work — up close and in tight. John Anderson's gonna be there and he's the favorite. You'll have to keep Piper in line to impress the judges — not that she needs to try."

Wesley nodded her head. She remembered the first trial, her shame and frustration. Now her room was covered in ribbons and photos — proof that she and Piper were among the best, proof that she had made the right choice when she took a chance on the little red merle that stormy November, almost two years ago. But how would Kyle feel about her competing against his dad now? And what if Piper actually won?

» «

At the little farm, the trees buzzed with cicadas, their rasping saw rising in urgent crescendos, then sputtering and clicking to a close. A cool breeze rustled through the leaves. September was already threatening the languid days of summer.

Cassel was entering grade six. She was nervous about having a locker for the first time. She started dressing with more care, trying to emulate her older cousin.

Wesley was entering grade eight. She was a senior at her middle school. Her success with Piper over the summer ensured her a constant band of loyal subjects, eager to share her company.

But things were far from perfect: Kyle had decided

to go to the high school in Kingston.

"You're leaving me behind," Wesley said, trying to hold back the tears.

"They have a good hockey team there," Kyle explained. "You know how important this is to me. I'm going to live with my uncle. I'll call you whenever I can."

Wesley turned away. "But I barely saw you all summer," she groaned. "Now we'll never see each other at all." She lowered her face, wiping the tears with her sleeve.

"It'll be okay, I promise," he reassured her. "I'll be home for Thanksgiving and Christmas, you'll hardly notice I'm not here."

Wesley nodded absently. "Sure. It'll be just fine," she mumbled, straightening her cap. She was used to being alone.

» «

When she wasn't thinking about Kyle, Wesley fretted endlessly about the impending trial. She spent her days in class dreaming of November. At night, after school, she would tend the biddies. When she was sure the hens were comfortable on their nests, she would grab Piper and run through their exercises.

One night, Wesley trudged behind the house, her black and red Wellingtons clumping over the frosty grass. Piper trotted happily beside her, nose held in the air. The night was cool and clear. Wesley exhaled, testing her breath against the cold. She could see the shimmering expanse of the Milky Way, spilling across the late October sky.

Piper suddenly stopped, her eyes focused across the yard. She gave a low, rumbling growl from the bottom of her throat.

"What's the matter, Pipes?" Wesley asked, looking down at the dog. "Seen a ghost?"

Piper lowered her head, rumbling louder. She stood motionless in the yard, unblinking eyes staring through the dark.

A loud crash caused an explosion of squawks from the chicken coop. Piper tore across the yard, barking furiously. From inside the coop, the biddies shrieked and squawked, their wings beating in terror against the walls.

"Piper!" Wesley screamed as the dog hit the chicken wire like a cannon ball.

Piper scrambled under the wire, barking and snarling ferociously.

Wesley stumbled after the dog. There were feathers on the ground and in the air. She heard the terrified squawks of the birds inside the coop.

And then she saw it, a silver phantom moving through the dark. It looked like a coyote, only bigger, with a wider skull and thicker legs. The fur bristled across its powerful shoulders as it zigzagged through the yard, a bloodied chicken swinging from its terrible jaws.

Wesley hurled her little pail with a shout, the pail coming down with a clatter behind the beast. It darted easily to one side — eyes flashing crimson in the light from the house — then disappeared suddenly, like a malevolent ghost in the night.

Piper snarled and barked, scrabbling under the chicken wire to the other side of the pen.

"Piper, no!" Wesley screamed.

The dog turned to look at her, her eyes lit with a wild, instinctive rage.

"Piper, down!" Wesley shouted.

The dog dropped to the ground. Wesley jumped over the fence, grabbing Piper by the collar. The chickens clucked and squawked in the coop.

Aunt Cindy appeared running, a flashlight jiggling in her hand.

"I saw it," Wesley howled. "It was big and white, like a wolf. It wasn't even afraid of me."

"Coydog," Aunt Cindy said, sucking in her breath. She hopped over the wire fence and stuck her head in the coop. The biddies blinked nervously back, their terrified eyes reflected in the light. "We'll have to make this hole smaller," she said, flashing the light on the opening to the coop. "I'll get Uncle Norman to do it in the morning."

Wesley knelt on the ground, Piper held firmly in her arms. Aunt Cindy inspected the chicken wire at the back of the coop. It was bent and misshapen where the killer had made its escape. She reached down and adjusted the wire, pulling it straight and tight across the posts. "It won't come back tonight," she promised, brushing the dirt from her hands.

# 13.

## THE NATIONALS

 The day was gray and somber. There was a tension in the air, palpable and contagious. A dark ridge of clouds hung in the sky.

People were bundled in mitts and thick wool sweaters, huddled in tight groups along the bleachers. The smell of decaying leaves and barbecue mingled together. The voice on the loudspeaker boomed and echoed. A tireless dog worked a small group of sheep down the field, the handler whistling clear and high.

Wesley sat on the bottom bleacher, Piper panting distractedly by her feet, Mr. Sharp's wooden crook tucked neatly under the bench. She wore her red bomber jacket over a blue sweater and a pair of loose-fitting jeans. Her long blonde hair hung in a pony tail from beneath her baseball cap. She clenched the whistle between her teeth, its familiar metallic taste on her tongue. She watched the dog drive the sheep into the pen. "One mistake," she muttered with a sigh.

The competition was good — very good. The Border Collies had finesse and intuition. They would be tough to beat. Wesley breathed in deeply, exhaling with a long, loud breath. Piper looked up with curiosity.

"Hope you're not as nervous as I am, girl," Wesley said, scrubbing the dog behind one ear. She turned her eyes back to the field. The next entrant was already at the marker. It was John Anderson and his Border Collie, Twist.

Twist had matured since Wesley saw her last. She was more focused and less skittish. Wesley pulled her lucky stone from her pocket, rubbing it methodically in her hand.

"Hey stranger," a cheerful voice said.

Wesley looked up to see Kyle's familiar face beaming down at her.

"Kyle!" she said, unable to hide her surprise. She tucked her lucky stone in her front pocket, then quickly turned away, spitting the whistle into her hand. "What are you doing here?" she asked, wiping her mouth with her sleeve.

If they had been alone, she would have jumped up and thrown her arms around him. But here, in front of everyone at the trial, she could only stare at him with awkward delight. "I can't believe you're here!" she said.

Kyle threw his head back and laughed, pleased that he had managed to surprise her. "I came for the trials today," he said. "My dad's running next." He pointed to the field and smiled openly, the gap showing between his teeth. "I thought you would be here."

Wesley looked down at the ground, the color rising in her face. She twisted her hair nervously with her fingers.

Rosemary and Aunt Cindy sat in folding chairs by the fence. Uncle Norman and Cassel leaned against the rail. Rosemary turned to look at her daughter. She wore a thick wool coat, the collar turned up around her neck. She held her hand over her eyes as though shielding the sun. She waved at Wesley, pointing at the field. Wesley nodded knowingly. Rosemary stared in her direction for a moment, then smiled and turned away.

"How are things at school?" Wesley asked, still twisting her ponytail.

"Okay." Kyle kicked the edge of the bleacher with his boot.

"Do you hate it and want to come home?" Wesley asked, smiling shyly, her eyes a smoky gray against the red of her jacket.

Kyle laughed again, playfully tugging Wesley's cap over her eyes.

The crowd broke into applause. Mr. Anderson

walked off the field, Twist trotting beside his leg.

"A near perfect run," the loudspeaker announced.

"You missed your dad's run," Wesley said.

Kyle shrugged, then smiled. "Oh well."

"I — I think I'm up next," Wesley stammered, bending over to pick up the crook. She adjusted her cap, pushing some stray hairs behind her ears. She squinted at Kyle from under her cap. "I might beat him, you know."

"Yeah. I don't know how I should feel about that," Kyle said.

Wesley looked at him for a moment, then nodded and made a motion as though to go.

Kyle quickly grabbed her hand. "Hey. Good luck," he whispered.

Wesley walked onto the field, Piper moving smoothly beside her. She turned to look at her mother who waved encouragingly from her seat by the fence. Kyle leaned against the rail next to Cassel, her yellow toque dangling carelessly from one hand.

The judge nodded. Wesley held her breath, her mind racing. She wished Mr. Sharp was there with his kind, round face and encouraging words. She felt the crook, cool and firm in her hand; she ran her fingers over the worn letters and tightened her grip. She could see the sheep, a small nervous bundle in the distance. Piper looked up at her expectantly, her head cocked to one side. Wesley flicked her hand.

The dog shot away and to the left, the white patch on her hind quarters flashing like the tail of a deer. Wesley whistled, high and far. Piper ran in a smooth, wide arc, then slowed to an even trot behind the sheep.

Kyle watched from the rail, Cassel staring coyly up at him.

"She's a lot better than she used to be, isn't she?" Cassel said, grinning.

Kyle nodded his head in agreement, his eyes trained on Wesley. Wesley stood at the marker, her face now calm and confident in the gray light. She held the crook out comfortably to one side.

"You love her, don't you?" Cassel asked, still staring up at Kyle.

Kyle turned to look at her, a surprised look on his face. He smiled broadly, then tousled Cassel's hair playfully with his hand.

Cassel kicked at the rail with the toe of her boot, the way she'd seen Kyle do. "I like the space between your teeth," she confessed shyly.

The sheep trotted through the third panel and down a small hill to the pen, Piper moving patiently behind. Wesley stood at the gate, crook outstretched. Piper scuttled to the left, head lowered, anticipating the sheep. The flock compressed then expanded, lurching into the pen all at once. Wesley closed the gate, fastening the rope to the post. Applause filtered through the air.

"Another perfect run for the little red merle from Picton," the loud speaker announced.

Wesley turned to see Kyle clapping, a wide grin on his face. His father was leaning on the rail next to the bleachers, shaking his head. Wesley ran toward the fence, just as Kyle leaped over the rail. Piper danced and barked excitedly around them as they walked from the ring together.

"You can't argue with a run like that!" Kyle said, laughing.

"It was good, wasn't it?" Wesley beamed. She stopped and looked at Kyle. "Can you stay for a while? I mean, with your dad and all."

Kyle glanced over to where his father was standing. His dad waved him to come over. Kyle just waved back. "Somebody had to beat him sometime," he said, matter-of-factly. "He's always complaining about the level of competition anyway. Are you hungry?"

Wesley nodded.

"Then let's get something to eat."

Wesley walked up to Cassel, handing her the leash. "Do you mind watching Piper? Kyle and I are going to get a hot dog."

"But I want a hot dog, too," Cassel protested.

Aunt Cindy grabbed Piper's leash, placing it in her daughter's hand. "You can get one with me in a minute," she said, shooting Cassel a look.

Wesley spent the rest of the day with Kyle, looking

at the displays, watching the other dogs on the field, and checking the standings on the slate board behind the bleachers. By the end of the day, Piper was in first place.

"You haven't beat us yet," Kyle said jokingly. "You have to win tomorrow to take the trophy."

Wesley looked up at Kyle. "I really want to win," she confessed.

"I know," he said, taking her hand. "What time will you be here tomorrow?"

"8:30."

"I'll be here at 8:00."

By the time Wesley ran up to the car, everything was packed and ready to go. Cassel and Piper waited impatiently in the back seat.

"Take your time," Cassel muttered as Wesley bounced breathlessly into the car.

Aunt Cindy and Rosemary chattered in the front seat about the day and the events scheduled for the next morning.

"Do you know what this means?" Aunt Cindy exclaimed. "This is the National. It doesn't get any bigger than this — not in this country, anyway. If we win this one, it's going to change everything. An Aussie has never held the National title."

Uncle Norman nodded complacently, dreaming about the landscape as he drove. Rosemary said that everyone should go to bed early to ensure a healthy start the next day. Cassel moaned that she couldn't get up any earlier than she already did, while Piper rustled and turned in her crate, trying to get comfortable. Wesley stared out the window at the diminishing light, oblivious to everything except the beating of her own heart.

» «

At home there were chores to do. Wesley fed Piper in the kitchen before changing into her boots. She exchanged her red jacket for an old purple barn coat and Maple Leafs toque. She took the silver pail off the nail in the mud room and grabbed the yellow plastic flashlight that Aunt Cindy kept hanging from a string on one of the pegs. Then she whistled for Piper, who already waited expectantly at the mud room door.

Wesley stepped beyond the light that pooled from the window at the side door and snapped on the flashlight, its beam jiggling over the frozen ground. She trudged down the path to where the biddies waited, the silver pail bouncing against her leg. Piper trotted along beside her, sniffing the cold night air.

Something moved in the darkness across the yard. Wesley shone the light toward the fence, the beam exposing a white, woolly form in the distance. She clumped over to the fence, hopping over the rail to Mr. Sharp's yard, hitting the ground with a thump. Piper shimmied under the fence, her ice blue eyes glinting in the dark.

Wesley moved down the lane, shining the flashlight ahead of her feet. She climbed the first rung on the fence to Mr. Sharp's field, scanning the night like a search beam. The surprised faces of the sheep were caught in the light, their wide, round eyes unblinking. They shifted nervously, their breath curling steam into the air. The lambs huddled close to their mothers, pressing for warmth and security. Piper stood at the base of the fence, her eyes focused across the field.

"It's just the sheep," Wesley mused, dropping to the ground. She leaned over, placed the flashlight on the ground and pulled her socks up inside her boots. She patted Piper on the head, then grabbed the flashlight and began tramping up the lane to the chicken coop.

Piper stood at the base of the fence, looking out at the ghostly sheep.

"Come on, Pipes," Wesley called from the top of the lane.

Piper stared into the night, then turned and ran up the lane to where Wesley was standing.

Wesley opened the gate to the chicken pen, flashing the light toward the front of the coop. There was a new wooden plate fashioned by Uncle Norman, with a small hole covering the opening. It was held with four wing nuts and a hinge. Wesley clumped over to the feed bin, lifted the heavy lid, and filled the silver pail with grain. Then she bent down in front of the coop, twisted the wing nuts on the makeshift plate, and pulled the cover open, securing it with a hook. She stuck her head inside and called to the chickens, tapping lightly on the side of the pail. The birds blinked back into the light, clucking softly.

"Come on, girls," Wesley coaxed, tapping on the pail again.

The biddies only shifted on their nests, cocking their heads and blinking with nervous curiosity.

"Well, okay," Wesley said. "I'm not gonna make you come out and eat. But if I was Aunt Cindy, you biddies would have some explaining to do." She laughed softly, thinking about her aunt admonishing the chickens. She placed the pail in the middle of the coop. "Just in case you get hungry in the night."

She closed the plate, transforming the opening once again into a small, "chickens only" sized hole, then looked around for Piper.

"Pi-per."

The yard was dark and quiet.

"Pi-per," Wesley called again.

The chickens clucked uneasily inside the coop. Wesley flashed the light across the yard, then up toward the house. There was a sudden movement from Mr. Sharp's field. The sheep bleated nervously.

"Piper!" Wesley called across the yard.

In an instant the sheep were thundering across the field, their frantic cries filling the air. In the distance,

Piper could be heard, barking ferociously. Wesley leaped over the chicken wire, stumbling toward the rail fence. She could hear the dog barking and barking, the sheep bleating in terror.

"Piper!"

Wesley scrambled over the fence, the light jiggling and bouncing over the ground. She ran down the lane, her clumsy boots knocking against her shins.

The sheep ran in all directions, the sound of their hooves heavy and urgent. Wesley scaled the second fence, the light illuminating the terrified animals. They moved in and out of the beam, eyes rolling, feet stabbing at the air. Piper howled like a demon from the far end of the field.

"Piper, no!" Wesley shrieked, running into the field.

The sheep ran toward her, bucking and twisting. One slammed against her hip, knocking her to the ground. The flashlight bounced and flipped across the grass. Wesley covered her face with one arm, another sheep springing recklessly over top of her. She heard a frenzied bleat, and the sound of ripping flesh. Piper raged over the cries of the sheep.

Wesley grabbed the flashlight, tripping and stumbling as she ran toward the horrifying sounds. In the beam of light she saw one of the sheep, thrashing mechanically on its side, its face frozen in terror. Several feet from the animal stood Piper, her legs streaked with blood. The hair on her back bristled and quivered. She crouched with her head held low, her lips curled over bared teeth. She gave a low, rumbling growl.

"Piper!" Wesley yelled, but the dog did not move.

Wesley flashed the light beyond the sheep and caught the eyes of three snarling coyotes glinting in the dark. They crouched threateningly, their teeth shining. At the front of the pack stood the phantom coydog, its fur bristling across powerful shoulders. It licked its teeth, its lips curling menacingly back. Wesley leaned over slowly, the light trained on the beasts, her hand groping for a firm, cool stone. She righted herself, the stone held tightly in her hand. "Get back Piper," she whispered.

Piper stood her ground, the low rumble quickening.

In a flash of white, the coydog lunged. Wesley hurled the stone, clipping the beast in the side. The animal spun around with a snarl, its feet hitting Wesley's chest like two fists, knocking the breath from her lungs in a rush as she thumped to the ground. The coydog snapped and snarled, tearing at the sleeves of her coat as she flailed her arms in front of her face, the beam from the flashlight arcing wildly through the dark.

Piper rammed the animal in the side, slamming it to the ground with a scream. Wesley struggled to her feet as the coyotes flew on top of Piper, teeth slashing, jaws snapping at her legs and head. Piper twisted and snarled, the beasts lunging and swirling around her. The coydog pulled Piper down, the wounded sheep's legs beating rhythmically in the air behind them.

Wesley ran toward the beasts, throwing the flashlight with all her strength. "Get away from her!" she screamed. The light bounced against one of the coyotes, then went out.

Piper rolled across the ground, disappearing beneath the swirling forms.

A gunshot cracked through the dark. The animals froze. Another shot blasted and echoed. The phantom coydog spun around, then ran, the coyotes scrabbling after it into the night.

Piper lay in front of the now lifeless sheep, her limp, motionless body small and frail on the ground. Wesley stumbled and fell to her knees beside her, sobs choking her throat.

"Oh God. Oh no, no, no." She ran her hands across the dog, the blood slippery and warm on her fingers. "Get up, Piper," she cried, her body shaking. "Please get up."

The dog lay unmoving, her pink tongue pinched between her teeth.

"What in the name of thunder!" Mr. Sharp appeared, his rifle in one hand, a powerful flashlight in the other.

"She's dead!" Wesley screamed, looking up at him, her eyes wild with terror and rage. She crumpled forward, sobbing hysterically, her face buried in her hands.

Mr. Sharp placed his gun on the ground and

scooped the dog into his arms. "She's still breathing. Get up, Wesley!" he shouted. "Run home and call the vet. Tell her we're bringing Piper in right now!"

Wesley pounded up the lane, her boots beating rhythm with her heart. She burst into the kitchen, screaming for her aunt to call the vet. The family was huddled at the window, the gunshots rousting them from all parts of the house.

"What happened?!" Rosemary hollered, seeing blood on Wesley's face and the torn sleeves of her coat. She lunged across the kitchen toward her daughter.

Wesley choked and stammered, the tears flowing down her face. She told them about the phantom coydog and the sheep, and about Piper, lying in a pool of blood.

Aunt Cindy picked up the phone, frantically punching the numbers.

Mr. Sharp roared up to the house, Piper quivering on a blanket in the back of his truck. Wesley burst from the side door, Rosemary running behind her. They jumped into the truck next to the dog, Mr. Sharp barely waiting for them to sit down, before tearing out of the driveway. Wesley stroked Piper's head as they rattled and lurched along the road, shielding the dog's body from the wind.

» «

Dr. Voight was standing at the door when the truck

pulled up to the office. "I have the room set up in the back."

Mr. Sharp rushed in, Piper in his arms. He placed the dog gently on the shiny steel table.

"You'll have to wait in the front room," the doctor said solemnly.

Wesley sobbed against her mother's chest, her body shuddering violently. "She saved my life," she choked.

Rosemary held her close, rocking back and forth the way she used to do when Wesley was a baby. Mr. Sharp stared across the room, shaking his head in disbelief.

It seemed an eternity before the vet reappeared, her face tired and drawn. She rubbed her forehead in exhaustion, leaning against the door frame. "She's in bad shape — I'm not going to lie about that. I put over four hundred stitches in her. There's some internal damage. She's lost a lot of blood."

Wesley listened, her weary face like a mask.

"Is she going to be all right?" Rosemary asked tentatively.

The doctor exhaled loudly, shaking her head. "I don't know. We just have to wait and see. If she makes it through tonight, she may have a chance."

"You don't mind if we wait here, do you?" Rosemary asked.

Dr. Voight smiled faintly. "You can keep me company. I'm not going anywhere."

"How's your coffee, Doc?" Mr. Sharp said, lightening the mood.

"Terrible." The vet smiled, reaching for a stained carafe on top of the filing cabinet. "But it's guaranteed to be hot." She disappeared into the back room.

Rosemary stroked her daughter's hair, smoothing it with her hand. Wesley buried her face in her mother's lap. She drifted off to sleep, her body jerking with sudden little sobs, the scent of coffee filtering through the antiseptic smell of the office.

# 14.

## LOYALTY

 Wesley woke to a gentle tug on her shirt. Dr. Voight leaned over her, a weak smile on her face. "It's morning. I think Piper's going to be okay."

"Can I see her?" Wesley whispered.

The doctor nodded. Wesley followed her to the back room wiping the sleep from her eyes. Her mother and Mr. Sharp were already there, staring at the dog.

Piper lay in a cage near the floor. Her eyes were swollen and closed. She had stitches and bandages everywhere. There was a bag of solution hanging from her cage with a long tube that led to one leg, fastened with white surgical tape. The dog twitched and woofed in her sleep, her body convulsing.

"She's not out of the woods yet," the vet cautioned.

"But she made it through the worst part." She squeezed the bag, checking the volume of the fluid. "You folks had better go get cleaned up. My assistant is coming in later to relieve me."

Wesley looked at the doctor, her worried face ready to protest.

"I'll call you as soon as anything changes," the doctor reassured her.

» «

Aunt Cindy, Uncle Norman and Cassel were sitting at the table when Wesley and Rosemary walked through the door. They listened carefully as Rosemary explained what the doctor had told them.

"Kyle phoned," Uncle Norman said. "He said he was sorry. The phone's been ringing all morning. Seems the whole county knows about Piper."

"She's out of the competition," Cassel said solemnly.

Wesley turned and walked from the kitchen. She stepped mechanically up the stairs and into her bedroom, closing the door behind her.

Cassel crept up the stairs, stopping tentatively at the bedroom door. She could hear Wesley crying from inside the room.

"Wes," Cassel said, tapping lightly on the door. She listened intently. Wesley continued to cry. "Wes," she said again, opening the door a crack.

Wesley sat on the edge of her bed, rocking gently. She turned away, not looking at Cassel. "Leave me alone."

"Piper's gonna be okay," Cassel said soothingly. She stood at the door, staring at her cousin. "She can go in the competition next year, when she's better."

"Better?" Wesley seethed, turning around to face her cousin. "She'll never be better! Don't you get it? They tore her to pieces! She's finished. She'll never work again!"

"Don't say that," Cassel whined her face crumpling. "You don't know that."

"I'll tell you what I do know," Wesley continued. "I know that there are no pets on this farm. You said so yourself — you *and* your mother. I hate you both!" She collapsed on the bed, her face buried in the covers.

Cassel burst into tears, wailing loudly from the bedroom door.

Rosemary rushed up the stairs, her black hair tumbling over her shoulders.

"What's going on?" she demanded.

"Wesley said that Piper's finished and she hates meeee," Cassel howled, sinking to the floor.

"Oh no," Rosemary consoled her young niece. "That's not true at all."

"It *is* true, Mom!" Wesley wailed from her bed.

"You know it's true! She's never gonna get better. You saw her. You saw what they did!" She sobbed loudly, covering her face with her hands.

» «

A family meeting was called.

"The vet bills alone are going to kill us," Aunt Cindy sighed from her end of the table.

"Mr. Sharp asked if he could contribute to the bills," Uncle Norman spoke up. "He said he wants to help pay. He figures that coydog and its pack of coyotes would have killed more than one sheep if Piper hadn't been there — or worse." He looked knowingly over at Wesley.

Wesley glowered at the table, her lips tightly pursed. "What about Piper?" she asked without looking up.

Aunt Cindy looked at her niece. "Well, Dr. Voight said she was through the worst part."

"I mean after that," Wesley growled. "What's going to happen when she gets home?"

Her aunt blinked with confusion. "We'll help her get better, of course."

"What if she doesn't get better?" Wesley asked accusingly. "What if she can't work?"

Aunt Cindy sat back in her chair. Everyone turned to look at her, except Wesley, who stared unflinchingly at the table. "Well, you don't just get rid of a dog like that," she said at last. "I mean, maybe she can still have puppies, or something. There isn't a farmer from here to Vancouver who wouldn't fight for bloodlines like that."

"Why, yes," Rosemary said hopefully.

Wesley looked at her aunt, her mouth softening. Aunt Cindy scraped her chair back from the table and put her arms around her niece. "We all want Piper to come home," she said. Wesley hugged her aunt, her eyes closed, the tears glistening on her cheeks. "Thank you," she whispered softly.

# 15.
## COMING HOME

 There is a time when the sun re-affirms its grandeur, pouring sunlight, honey gold, for one last time, before winter drapes the earth in a thin, gray veil.

Cassel stood in the light, her face eager and impatient. "When are they gonna get here?" she asked.

"Soon," Norman said.

The car pulled up beside the house. Wesley jumped from the passenger seat and opened the back door. She held a long, leather leash in her hand. Aunt Cindy turned off the engine and got out of the car, walking over to the back where Wesley was standing. She reached in, fumbled for a moment, then stood up, Piper held in her arms. She placed the dog carefully on the driveway.

Piper stood, eyes squinting, uncertain legs trembling as she sniffed the air with curiosity. She was thin, and her coat was rough, with big bare patches where the vet had shaved for stitches. She limped along the driveway, squatting to pee in a small patch of grass.

Wesley trolled patiently beside her, holding the leash. She picked Piper up when they reached the stairs, carrying her gently into the kitchen. Piper wiggled happily when Cassel met her at the door.

Goblin was waiting on the windowsill. He leaned over to greet the dog, their noses touching in familiar greeting. They sniffed each other for a moment, then Piper groaned and turned away, limping to her crate. She thumped heavily down on the sheepskin liner, her eyes closed, licking her lips with satisfaction.

*A gentle breeze blows from the south. It runs warm fingers across the green, pushing the grasses to one side in shimmering waves, rolling out in rhythmic succession to the horizon. The lake glitters there, the sun dancing resplendent upon the water. The girl walks into the sun, the breeze brushing the hair from her face. A dog moves beside her, its steps deliberate and slow. The girl reaches out, the tips of her fingers touching the dog's ear, bright eyes shining in the light.*

# PIPER'S PEDIGREE

CH. Blue River City Slicker OTDC. ATDS. **"Slick"**

WTCH Blue River Motown Slick **"Sly"**

Stay Steady's Powder Puff **"Puff"**

CH. Las Manos Cadillac Jack OTDC. ATDCSD. **"Jack"**

Little Rock's Lester **"Lester"**

Little Rock's Lena ATDSD. OTDC. **"Lena"**

Little Rock's Cornflower STDC. **"Blue"**

**Triblue's Spitfire OTDD. ATDS. "Piper"**

CH. Macado's Crazy Horse CDX. STDC. OTD. **"Teak"**

CH. Stardancer's Still Crazy CD. STDSD. **"Drum"**

CH. Macado's Chili Pepper **"Chili"**

CH. Evergreen's Wind Chimes Cdn & ASCA Champion **"Holly"**

CH. Still Water's Bring Em Back Jack CD. **"JJ"**

Beauregarde's Dancing in the Dark **"Brie"**

CH. Beauregarde's Silver City Cabaret **"Silver"**

Breed: Australian Shepherd      Color: Red Merle    Sex: Female
Whelped: November 24, 1997      Breeder: Evergreen/Triblue

| | | |
|---|---|---|
| STD Started Trial Dog | S Sheep | CH. Conformation Champ |
| OTD Open Trial Dog | D Ducks | CD Companion Dog (Obedience) |
| ATD Advanced Trial Dog | C Cattle | CDX Companion Dog Excellent |
| WTCH Working Trial Champ | | (Obedience) |

## AUTHOR'S NOTE

 Although the exact lineage of the Australian Shepherd is unknown, it is believed that they are Spanish in origin, not Australian as the name suggests. Interestingly, it is the Basques, a people of equally unknown origin living around the Western Pyranees in France and Spain, who are credited with introducing the hearty little dogs to Australia and North America. Because the Basques have no written language, and speak a language that is neither Spanish nor French, there is no record of the dog's actual origin. What we know of the Australian Shepherd has been passed down from word of mouth and through legends. Early documentation is in the form of photographs and paintings dating back to the 1800s. But the Basque people brought the dogs with them wherever they went to herd sheep and are historically linked to the present-day Australian Shepherd.

In the late 19th century many Basques immigrated to Australia in search of work, successfully establishing themselves and their dogs as shepherds in the outback. When American sheep stock was aggressively upgraded with Australian sheep in the early 1900s, the Basques traveled with the animals to the New World, bringing with them their "little blue dogs" — a name referencing the Australian Shepherd's characteristic blue merled coat. It is believed that the dogs had already unofficially arrived in North America in 1493 with Christopher Columbus, but it wasn't until this time that they were formally introduced to the US — which undoubtedly explains the origin of their present-day breed name, the "Australian" Shepherd.

The Australian Shepherd is recognized as a dependable herding dog of superior stamina and intelligence, willing to give his life to protect the family and possessions of his owner. His natural ability and versatility allows him to shine in many arenas, including performing as trick dogs in rodeos, in obedience, agility and herding trials, at Frisbee competitions, and in the field as a stock dog. He is as adaptable as the situation allows, successfully herding different types of stock like ducks, sheep and cattle. Australian Shepherds have even been used to herd buffalo in some national parks.

The Australian Shepherd is classified as a "loose-eyed" herding dog, which means he does not use an intense stare to intimidate and control the stock as some "eye" dogs do, like the Border Collie. While there are varying degrees of "eye" in both breeds, most "eye" dogs are typically silent, exhibiting more slinking and creeping behavior. Australian Shepherds, on the other hand, herd in an upright position and sometimes use their bark as a means of control—although excessive barking is considered a sign of inexperience. Aussies are masters at working in close but can work at a distance as well, and it is acceptable for them to use their mouths to "grip" the stock when necessary. Border Collies prefer the open field, and rarely use their grip. They also do a lot of stopping and dropping, whereas the Aussie generally moves more, stopping when told. These differences in herding styles often lead people to champion one breed over the other.

The most characteristic trait of the Australian Shepherd is his natural bobtail. While not all Aussies are born with a bob, it has been accepted as the breed standard. Thus puppies born with tails are usually "docked" to within four inches or less.

Essentially, the breed comes in black or red, with many variations on these two themes: solid black or red, with or without white and/or tan or copper points; blue merle (sometimes called "salt and pepper"), which is a modification of the basic black body with a combination of powder blue, silver blue, steel gray or blue black; and red or "liver" merle (also called "cinnamon and sugar"), a combination of liver, burgundy, shades of rust, and/or sorrel. Merle coloring can be bold and contrasting to evenly blended, with patterns varying from roan, to flecked, freckled (or mottled), to marbled, splotched and patched. Both red and blue merles can have white points as well. Red is a recessive gene, which means that both parents must carry the red gene in order for some of the pups to show this color.

The eyes of the Australian Shepherd are as unique as their coats and can be any combination of blue, brown, and/or amber, with some individuals possessing one eye of each color. Marbled eyes combining several colors, are characteristic of merles, although any eye combination is possible.

As seen in Jeanne Joy Hartnagle's *All About Aussies,* Alpine Publications Inc., Loveland, Colorado, 1985.